Something About Ginger

A Novel By

J. Monique Gambles

It's BOLD Publishing
Published by It's BOLD Publishing
P.O. BOX 914
Desoto Texas 75123-0914

© Copy Right 2010
All rights reserved

Printed in the United States of America
Without limiting the rights under copyright reserved above, no part of this publication may be reproduced, stored in or introduced into a retrieval system, or transmitted, in any form, or by any means (electronic, mechanical, photocopying, recording, or otherwise), without the prior written permission of both the copyright owner and the above publisher of this book.
BOOKS ARE AVAILABLE AT QUANTITY DISCOUNTS WHEN USED TO PROMOTE PRODUCTIONS OR SERVICES. FOR INFORMATION PLEASE WRITE TO MARKETING DIVISION, IT'S BOLD PUBLISHING P.O. BOX 914 DESOTO TX 75123-0914
If you purchased this book without the cover you should be aware that this book is stolen property. It was reported as "unsold and destroyed" to the publisher and neither the author nor the publisher has received any payment for this "stripped book.

Also By J. Monique Gambles

Saturday's Epiphany: Reflections

When the Drama Has Ceased

Special thanks to the person, whom I truly loved but gave me so much grief—fueling my anger, pushing me to write, write, write!

Foreword

"Who can you trust when you can't trust the ones you love, or yourself?
--- Try trusting God."
   J.

Part I:

The Honeymoon

Chapter One

"Honey, you know, I had the strangest dream last night," Mackenzie told Julian, as they sat closely on the airplane returning from their month-long honeymoon in St. Croix.

"Really? What about? You know, we only had a couple of hours of sleep," Julian replied, touching the bottom of her lip.

She smiled back at Julian with a flirtatious grin. "I know, but I was still able to dream what seemed like a series of dreams. I woke up at one point but didn't bother to wake you. You seemed to be sleeping soundly, kind of breathing in and out, in a rhythm."

Mackenzie mimicked him for a moment and Julian laughed. Shaking his head, he said, "Who, me?"

They kissed in between laughs and Mackenzie, startled, looked at the flight attendant, who had an obvious, worried look, on her face. Julian, who sensed Mackenzie's concern, followed her gaze to the flight attendant, who had begun to fan herself.

The tall, fair-complexioned flight attendant with the crop cut was flustered as she reached for the microphone set to give an announcement. But, before she could get a word out, she was whisked away by another short, full-figured flight attendant, and they vanished into the corridor. They talked in what sounded like muffled whispers and sobs.

"Something's wrong," Mackenzie said.

"I think you're right. I'd better go ask what's going on."

Julian began to unfasten his seat belt and excused himself. He proceeded to find the flight attendants while the other first class patrons either sipped on fine wine, played with their laptops, or dosed off into Never-Never Land.

He reached the corridor of the plane, next to the pilots' section, and saw that the two flight attendants were wiping their eyes.

"Umm, excuse me, but uh, my wife and I were wondering if everything is okay. Is there something we need to know? Like if this plane is going to land safely," he asked, with a puzzled look on his face.

The two flight attendants looked at each other, then looked at Julian. "Sir," the tall one said, as she cleared her throat, "there seems to be a state of emergency nationwide. The FAA is asking that we not land this plane but divert to Canada. That's all I can tell you."

"Wait a minute. What do you mean national security? What's going on?" Julian asked. He was looking for answers and not some drummed up speech they were going to concoct.

With a look of empathy, the tall flight attendant spoke earnestly. "Sir, we can't give out any more information because we are unsure. They have informed the pilot that we cannot land on U.S. soil until given clearance. I'm sorry, sir."

Julian looked at the two women who offered support to one another by holding hands and asked that they keep him posted. They agreed. Flustered, he went back to his seat.

"You're right, hon, something is wrong, but they're not saying. All they told me was that they can't land the plane on U.S. soil." Julian knew not to tell Mackenzie about the state of emergency for fear that Mackenzie would become worried. He knew that that kind of information had better come with explicit details, and he had none to give.

"They can't land the plane. That's not good. What about the fuel? We may run out," Mackenzie said, trying not to sound worried.

In the back of her mind, her dreams were coming clear to her.

"So, what did you dream about?" Julian asked, trying to get her mind off their situation.

"Oh, well it was weird. Sam and Red were both in it but then they just disappeared when we were at church. I kept looking all over for them but it was like I was going around in circles. Then Lauren finds me at the church, and she's crying telling me she was worried about me."

"Was I in it?" Julian asked quizzically.

"We were together at first, then I leave—that's when I meet up with Sam and Red at the church, and by the way, we are talking, but I have no idea what was said. I'm telling you, it was weird. But very graphic."

Julian looked attentively at Mackenzie and grabbed her hand. "It does sound weird, but I'm sure everything is okay. We can call Lauren as soon as we land."

Mackenzie held Julian's hand and turned to the window. She realized that worry would be her worst enemy. She decided to catch up on her rest. She and Julian had tons of things to do as a married couple. First and foremost, they had to find a new home in California now that Julian had decided to team up with his old friend and Mackenzie's old flame, Ken, to start up a firm in San Francisco. But just as she began to fall asleep, the pilot began making an announcement.

"Good morning, ladies and gentlemen," the mild-spoken, unseen pilot said before clearing his throat. "American Airlines would like to thank you for choosing our airline, and we welcome you to fly again with us in the very near future. We would like to bring to your attention that the FAA has issued a warning and request that we land in Canada. While we cannot give any specifics, we would like to assure you that there aren't any safety issues with this plane. Please do not be alarmed; we assure you that THERE ARE NO PROBLEMS WITH THE PLANE. This was just sent to us from the FAA. Once again, this flight will be headed to Canada; we will not be landing at John F. Kennedy airport. Thank you, and thanks for flying American Airlines."

The first class passengers began to sit upright, visibly concerned. There was an older guy with a deep Italian accent that asked, "Uh, wat do ya mean? This is insane. My wife is supposed to pick me up from the airport at noon. What's going on here?"

"Sir, we are sorry for the inconvenience, but with all the news going on, I'm sure your wife will know that your plane won't be landing in New York at noon," the shorter flight attendant said.

The slightly balding man was agitated but at a lost for words. He, along with the other passengers, looked around in search of more information or group cohesiveness to get to the bottom of their ordeal. Julian and Mackenzie continued to hold hands and wait for further word.

Mackenzie knew something was terribly wrong—something that involved her loved ones, something that made her knees weak—and she thought of using the restroom, but she decided to wait so she wouldn't miss anything.

Julian couldn't wait. He excused himself as Mackenzie sat quietly and prayed; trying to put her dreams out of her mind.

Sam was married to Natalie now, and they had been expecting their first child. Maybe the dream had something to do with Natalie having the baby sooner than she thought, and Sam had to leave in a hurry—or Lauren was worried about leaving Mackenzie in St. Croix with Julian.

After all, the two of us back together and deciding to get married on a whim would make anyone worry after they found out why we broke up in the first place, Mackenzie thought to herself.

Julian returned to his seat and grabbed Mackenzie's hand. She turned back to the window and forced herself to catch up on her sleep.

She knew getting back to the States meant doing a lot of work. She had to arrange to get her things from Atlanta; and Julian had to arrange to sublease his condo in Dallas. Then there was Jay-Jay—she still had to get her back.

Mackenzie was ready for a change and used that energy to forget what was going on now. And although she and Ken had shared a brief kiss so many years ago, she was delighted that he and Julian would be working together. This was going to give her a chance to do some independent work as well.

She pictured the four of them all newly weds, new to the area, and ready to take San Francisco by storm. She drifted off to sleep in anticipation of her new life.

Chapter Two

"Mackenzie, Mackenzie, wake up, baby. Come on, we can get off and stretch our legs while they refuel," Julian quietly whispered to Mackenzie, who was now sound asleep. "Baby, wake up. Let's go stretch and get something to eat."

Mackenzie yawned a little and stretched. She turned to Julian and spoke softly, saying, "Are we home yet? I need to call Lauren."

Julian gave her a light kiss on her forehead. "We're in Canada, remember? But they did say we could get out and stretch and grab a bite. We'll have to report back to the plane in an hour or so."

"Well, I have got to call Lauren." Mackenzie hurried off the plane, with Julian following close behind her.

They walked through the airport hand in hand and noticed that many of the people were glued to the TV monitors as though something catastrophic was going on.

"Hon, let's check it out, see what's on the news. Maybe we can find out why we are in Canada and not home by now," Mackenzie said.

"Are you sure? We can just wait until we get home. We probably won't be able to see anyway."

"Honey, you do realize that we are in Canada against our will, without any definite information as to why? Of course I want to know what's going on."

While Mackenzie slept peacefully on the plane, Julian had already found out about the attacks on New York City, the Pentagon, and about the plane going down in Pennsylvania. He knew that the World Trade Center towers were merely dust by now.

He didn't want to worry Mackenzie because her whole family and many of her close friends were in New York City. Some may have even worked at the World Trade Center.

"Come on, I want to know why this plane is here and not in New York, or better yet, why I'm not home by now—or close to it."

She pulled Julian, laughing at his stubbornness, and made her way to one of the monitors.

"Oh my God," Mackenzie gasped, covering her mouth with one hand and holding her stomach with the other.

What she saw was people leaping out of the World Trade Center just before the buildings crumbled to the ground and a plane slamming into the Pentagon. It was a recast of the day's earlier events.

"Julian, do you see this? Oh my God!" Mackenzie began to cry out at the top of her lungs.

"Baby, calm down; get a hold of yourself. Please, we'll call as soon as the lines are clear. I promise."

She was distraught; she did not hear a word that he said. Mackenzie frantically searched for a phone and left Julian; who tried to catch up to her. He found her a few gates down trying to get other frantic callers off the phone so she could use it.

When she couldn't find a phone, she began to scream again. Julian grabbed her and held her until she calmed down. The entire airport was still with melancholy, and Mackenzie's screams echoed throughout as others stood by and fought back tears or paced impatiently, awaiting further notice.

"Baby, the phones are all tied up. I promise, we will stop in New York and go see your family before we do anything. I promise. Even if we have to take a cab or a city bus—I'll get you to your family."

Those words seemed to fall on deaf ears because Mackenzie couldn't make sense of anything. She knew her whole family was in New York. Lauren worked not too far from the WTC site, and Sam worked in

Tower II on the 85th floor. And there she was, stuck in Canada indefinitely, not able to reach either of them.

The Canadian airport security arrived and tried to offer help, but Julian explained their situation and just asked that they help get her back on the plane so he could get her to her family. He knew Mackenzie was hurting, and there wasn't much he could do.

Once they returned to the plane, the passengers were informed that the airports were shut down in the U.S., and they would not be heading back to the States until further notice. That meant they would be spending the night in Canada—a plan that neither she nor Julian expected.

The same Italian man was visibly upset and began holding his chest and gasping for air. He was not alone, as those words seemed to trigger a sense of chaos on the huge 757 Boeing aircraft.

Sighs, moans, grunts, and sudden movement erupted all at once.

Julian knew that a stay in Canada wasn't news that Mackenzie wanted to here, but to his surprise, she told him that they had better start looking for a room before all the rooms by the airport were taken.

They exited the plane hurriedly and picked up their luggage, then checked with the airline about further instructions before heading to the nearest Marriott across the freeway from the airport.

Mackenzie moved along with Julian, still not saying anything. It was as if she was drifting along.

She sat quietly in the lounge while Julian spoke to the receptionist and reserved their room. Inside, Mackenzie looked through their luggage and took out her toiletries, along with her silk pajama short set to sleep in.

She went into the bathroom and locked herself in, turned on the shower water, making sure it was set to the hottest temperature, and as the steam filled the bathroom, Mackenzie cried. Her world was coming to an end.

She knew her dreams meant something, and the terrorist attacks were just an indication that someone close to her was no longer around. But the question that was running through her mind was who? *Who was she going to lose this time?*

Julian softly knocked on the door. "Honey, won't you open up and let me in?" He knew what Mackenzie was going through. She had already lost a lot in life. She had finally told him her entire life story—even the truth about her mother's death at the hands of some of the patients at the hospital. She had told him about her father's silent struggle with his addictions and AIDS before finally dying of a heart attack, or what she liked to believe to be a broken heart. And she told him of the abuse she'd suffered, causing her to act out sexually, which she'd blamed herself for, for many years.

"Julian, I just want to be alone right now," Mackenzie said through the door, trying to clear the sound of tears from her voice. "I promise, I'm okay."

"Baby, please," the green-eyed, half-dressed Julian pleaded, knowing that his wife needed him.

"Mackenzie, please," he called again, holding back his own tears.

The door opened slightly as he slid his credit card against the lock and turned the knob. Julian walked in, feeling powerless, and found Mackenzie kneeling down by the toilet, her face red and tears strolling with her mascara everywhere, like she had tried to wipe her tears away in a hurry.

Julian walked over to her, stroked the side of her face, and wiped away her tears before helping her stand up. "Mackenzie baby, let me help you out of your clothes and get you cleaned up. Come on now."

She struggled out of her clothes and mumbled, "Someone's dead. I know it. I just have to find out who?"

"Sweetie, we don't know that yet, but as soon as we can get back, I'm sure everything will be okay. I promise you. I told the airline where we were staying and gave them both of our cell phone numbers. As soon as we hear something, we're going straight to New York."

Mackenzie ran her hands through her hair and nodded her head to Julian's caring words.

She thought for a moment about Julian insisting on the two of them taking their cell phones on their honeymoon and the fact that she'd disagreed. It wasn't until the second week into the honeymoon that she'd stopped fussing about it, since Julian was able to get the deal with Ken and make arrangements about their firm in San Francisco. It had paid off having the cell phones—especially on a day like today, she thought.

"Maybe they will be working again by tomorrow. Better yet we can call Lauren and Sam. How's that?" Julian asked as Mackenzie thought about Lauren while getting undressed.

He undressed as well and they showered together. Julian washed her hair, and her entire body, then sat her down on the side of the tub and shaved her legs as she massaged and rinsed his bald head.

After their shower, they dried each other off, climbed into the bed, and Julian held her while she silently cried herself to sleep.

Chapter Three

They awoke early the following morning. The airline had called them at the hotel to inform them that they could catch the earliest flight into New York, which was 11:00 am that morning. They could be in New York by 3:00 at the latest.

They skipped breakfast and prepared to leave. Julian had dressed quickly and went downstairs to check out while Mackenzie packed up her toiletries and tried to do something with her hair, which was tangled to no end.

As she combed through the tangles, staring into the mirror in the bathroom, she thought about trying to reach Lauren again. Her insides were going crazy because she had no answers. She put down her comb and decided to give it a try.

Her hands shook as she dialed the numbers. And after several clicks, and confirmation from the operator, the phone rang. Just as it was about to go to the second ring, her younger brother Aaron picked up.

"Hello?"

"Hey, little brother, what are you doing?" Mackenzie said, trying not to sound worried.

"Mackenzie, you okay? Where you at? Lauren and Erica have been buggin' worrin' 'bout you. Ya'll still on the islands?"

Mackenzie breathed a sigh of relief when her little brother said both her sisters' names.

"You won't believe it but we are in Canada and headed to New York this morning. They wouldn't let us land anywhere in the U.S. yesterday."

Aaron's voice suddenly turned low. "So, you heard, huh? That shit is fucked up. See, doz nigga's always sayin' it's the black man, lockin' us up for everything under the sun and it's doz Indian mutha fuckas they let com ova here for free. Ain't that a bitch?"

"Yeah, it is something to ponder. But we haven't watched the news yet. After I saw those people jumping out of windows and planes crashing into buildings, I was through."

They were both silent for a moment.

"You talked to Sam?" Aaron asked, like he knew something was up.

"No, but I know he worked down there," Mackenzie replied, trying to hold back her tears.

"Well, hold up, let me get Lauren."

For a moment, Mackenzie felt relieved again because she knew that Lauren was okay.

"Hey you, what's up, girl?"

"Hey Lauren, how are you? Everything okay?"

Lauren sighed deeply and said, "Girl, you just don't know; I'm ready to leave this shit hole—people falling out the sky and shit. God, I get goose bumps thinking about it. That shit shook me up. And when we couldn't reach you, a sister was broke down. You here me? Booga's and snot ova here wit Erica. Shit!"

"Well, is everyone accounted for yet?" Mackenzie asked, as Julian knocked on the door. She realized that he'd turned in the room keys.

"Yeah, just about—"

"Hang on, Lauren, let me open the door for Julian; he had to turn in the keys." Mackenzie put down the receiver and quickly walked to the door, motioned in Julian, and mouthed Lauren's name before she picked back up the phone.

"Okay sis, I'm back. So, everyone is accounted for then, right?"

"The family is all good. Aunt Michelle was down there but escaped the first building falling down. She walked up to my job all out of breath, scaring the shit out of me, covered in soot. Nigga almost gave me a heart attack. You know how dramatic she is."

Mackenzie sighed again.

"Did you know anyone that worked in either of the buildings? 'Cause those shits are dust now."

Mackenzie thought about Sam and his plush job on the 85th floor. She thought of how proud he had been for finally putting his schooling and degree to work. He was paid, about to be a father, and married to the beautiful Natalie. She remembered how happy they'd looked at the wedding—the huge house that was elegantly decorated and how all of his friends came up to Long Island to wish him and Natalie well.

"Mackenzie, you still there?"

"Girl, I'm sorry—just thinking about Sam. He worked in one of the buildings; I'm just not sure which one. God, did they say there were any survivors? I mean, what are they saying?"

"I guess you haven't watched the news then, 'cause it's all on there. They say that when the planes hit, the fire probably killed people instantly, and the buildings probably crushed the people that were trying to escape when they fell down."

Mackenzie looked over at Julian, who was listening attentively. "Well, that's not good, unless Sam was late for work, like he used to be for church. Maybe I should call his folks."

Lauren coughed for a second as she took a drag off of her cigarette then responded to Erica, who was going non-stop in the background. "Yeah, Erica, they fine. Damn girl, get a grip. We're talking about Sam. Her and Julian are in Canada. Would you shut up so we can finish talking?"

"Tell her I'm fine, and Julian's fine. We're trying to get there now."

"You hear dat, nosy, they are on their way here." Lauren huffed to Erica.

"Okay, won't you give me Sam's number or his grandmother's number, and I'll call and check, and when you get here, I'll have all the information. Just stop worrying and get here."

Mackenzie gave her Sam's grandparent's number and hung up the phone.

"Everything okay?" Julian asked. Mackenzie blew out hard and walked over to Julian. She grabbed his hands and wrapped them around her waist.

"Lauren said the family is all accounted for, and she said she would call Sam for me. By the time we make it there, she should be able to tell me something."

"Well that's great, Mackenzie," Julian said, after kissing her softly on the forehead. "Come on, we'd better get going if we're going to catch that plane."

"Yeah, you're right—I just need to pull my hair up and I'm ready. It'll just take me a few seconds."

"Okay, I'll start taking everything downstairs." They kissed and Mackenzie disappeared into the bathroom as Julian began taking down their luggage.

Chapter Four

The anxiety that had filled Mackenzie's head was finally letting up. Speaking to Lauren and Aaron was like a breath of fresh air. She was even anticipating a long, hearty talk with Sam once she made it to New York.

The transition to board the plane went smoothly, and they discussed their plans to relocate to San Francisco once they left New York. They agreed that it would be much better to have Mackenzie's things professionally packed and moved after they picked out a house; and while she set up in San Fran, Julian could go back to Dallas and finalize leasing out his condo.

The new firm that Julian and Ken were starting didn't require much setting up because Julian was already known in the business and had quite a bit of inquiries. Ken had already picked out the spot and was interviewing clerks and had a couple of secretaries already lined up.

The flight into New York's LaGuardia airport went smooth, aside for a little anxiety for a handful of flyers. Mackenzie and Julian sipped on their favorite glasses of Kendall Jackson and talked to avoid worrying about the plane. Before they knew it, it was time for their plane to land.

The airport in New York was filled with National Guardsman, and the stillness in the air was nothing less than sorrowful. They picked up their luggage and walked hand in hand through the crowds of saddened faces that searched for answers but could find none. Some even spoke, greeting each other as if to stand in solidarity, something Mackenzie knew had never existed in New York City. One of the reasons why she'd stayed away so many years was because of the harshness and fast-paced living of its rude inhabitants.

Mackenzie spotted Aaron leaning against the wall, talking on his cell phone. He had a do-rag on with an oversized sweatshirt, baggy jeans, and new Timberland boots, which were half laced.

When he spotted Mackenzie, he ended his called and hurried over with outstretched arms to greet her.

"What's up, big sis?"

"Hey you. Man, you just keep getting taller."

He smiled and kissed her on the forehead once they'd hugged.

"Aaron, this is my husband Julian. Julian, this is one of my younger brother's, Aaron, aka Pretty." She smiled, poking Aaron in his side. Aaron smiled and extended his hand, and the two greeted each other.

"Aaron, why do you insist on wearing those baggy clothes?" Mackenzie asked, as Aaron posed for a second, then laughed.

"'Cause the ladies love it."

"Yeah okay. So now we're calling 'skeeza's' ladies. Wow, times have really changed."

"Very funny. Come on, I got my ride out front wit my boyz."

"Well, we can rent a car."

"Come on, big sis. I got you."

Mackenzie looked at Julian and he smiled, agreeing with Aaron. They headed to Aaron's car.

The all-black Honda Accord with tinted windows, flashy rims, and a spotless exterior was filled with smoke as Aaron opened the doors and told his friends, "Yo, my man, put dat out, son."

Julian and Mackenzie shared another look and smiled because it was obvious that it wasn't the smell of cigarettes that filled the air.

Aaron popped the trunk as cars passed and people met, greeted, and left in and out of the busy airport. Even after yesterday's plane crashes, people still had places to be. *Typical of New Yorkers*, Mackenzie thought.

Julian and Aaron loaded the trunk while Mackenzie watched. Then they did some rearranging of the seats, and they all crammed into Aaron's car.

"Yo, dis is my sistah, Mackenzie, and my brother Julian. And deeze are my boyz, Mike and Bal."

Mackenzie and Julian waved hi like twins and held hands afterward in between knee nudges because the smell of weed was intoxicating.

But with the police officers being so busy with the disaster inside lower Manhattan, their trip to Brooklyn would be a breeze. Surely the cops would have better things to do than stop a car full of black folks. *After all, it wasn't us that committed the crime.* Mackenzie kept trying to convince herself as Aaron sped through the city streets.

The music that played in the background, a mixed tape of Notorious BIG, gave her a bit of a New York edge as she bopped her head a little and anticipated her meeting with Sam.

"Yo, you talked to Lauren yet?"

"No, not since we all talked earlier today."

"Oh. Aight. Well, umm. Let me make one stop before we get there. That cool?"

"Yeah, sure." Mackenzie snuggled closer to Julian and continued looking out of the window through the tinted glass.

In her mind, she was preparing for their move to San Fran. She was excited about picking out a brand new house with Julian and starting life over again.

Finally, she was freed of her past. She could only think of the good things in life, like her husband Julian, the closeness she was finally experiencing with her family, and her new life ahead in sunny California and reuniting with Jay-Jay.

Aaron dropped off his friends and then proceeded to Lauren and Erica's apartment; zipping through the sporadic Brooklyn traffic.

The same brownstone that they had all gathered at when Jun passed had a warm, welcoming scent that bloomed from behind the door. Julian and Aaron unloaded the car and took the things upstairs while Mackenzie followed along.

Aaron searched for his keys in the tiny hallway and became flustered when he couldn't find them. Finally, he shouted to his other siblings, "Yo, open the door. I can't find my keys."

Mackenzie and Julian laughed at her brother's absentmindedness and waited patiently for Lauren to open the door.

Lauren was saying obscenities when she swung open the door and plucked Aaron on his forehead.

"Quit smoking so much," she said, then turned her attention to Mackenzie and Julian.

"Hi newlyweds. My tan is gone already—cheap Caribbean sun. Shoot, I thought I would be able to sport it 'til at least October sometime." She laughed at herself as she spat out her thoughts.

"Yo, I'm sayin' let us in—deeze bags is heavy," Aaron stated, as Lauren rolled her eyes.

"You still here, rock egg?" she said, then stepped to the side as they all walked in.

"Where's Erica and the kids?"

"The mall. He needs new shoes and she needs a new dress."

"Who does? Erica?" Mackenzie asked, as she and Julian walked into the cluttered living room filled with toys and CDs.

"Yeah girl, but anyway. Sit down and rest your feet. Julian, would you like something to drink? We have water, Pepsi, Heineken, and some white wine Erica brought home from her boss's housewarming last week."

"Oh sure. I'll have some Pepsi."

"Okay. And I know you want water, Mackenzie. You kill me with this healthy attitude you have adapted."

"Girl, I need water like your brother needs his special cigarettes."

"Okay." Lauren chimed then disappeared into the kitchen while the turning of the doorknob startled Mackenzie, who was attempting to take off her shoes and relax on the couch with Julian.

When the door opened, Mackenzie's niece and nephew burst through, playing tag as Erica struggled in with shopping bags and muttered to her children—who were obviously not paying her any attention.

"Hey, girl"

"Mackenzie, hi. Let me set these bags down."

Mackenzie stood, anxious to hug her oldest sister as Julian stood as well, like the proper gentleman.

Erica placed the bags on the floor and reached out and gave Mackenzie a warm hug. "Sorry about Sam," she said. "He was a nice guy. I know you will miss him."

Mackenzie pulled back with an unclear look on her face, shaking her head in confusion.

"Yeah, I just took the kids to get something to wear to the funeral," Erica said, looking away, not paying attention to the obvious. This was news to Mackenzie.

When she looked up and saw the look on Mackenzie's face, Lauren walked in and rolled her eyes, shaking her head.

"I didn't tell her yet, numb numb!"

"Tell me what?" Mackenzie asked, still shaking her head like she was refusing to accept the information.

"I don't understand," she said, as Julian began to reach for her hand.

"No, what are you talking about? Tell me what you mean, Erica."

Erica and Lauren looked at each other, and her niece and nephew stopped playing, sensing the sudden change in mood.

Julian reached for his wife again, but she snapped at him, "No Julian. I want to know what's going on here. Tell me what, Lauren? Say it. I want to know what you are talking about."

"Mackenzie," Lauren said, in her nonchalant tone. "Mackenzie, calm down." She paused again. "They can't find Sam. He went to work yesterday to meet up with what's his name. Red, I believe that's what his grandmother said. And they can't find either of them."

"They what? They what?" Mackenzie asked. Her breath began to quicken and she felt like she was losing her composure.

"Honey, come on, get a hold of yourself."

"Get a hold of myself?" she yelled at Julian. "It's not your friends! It's not your friends dying!" she yelled. Tears fell as she was hit with the truth.

Lauren, Erica, and the kids looked on as Mackenzie turned to Julian, and he consoled her. She cried tears of hurt and thoughts of abandonment reflected in the back of her mind. She wondered how many more people she would lose.

"I'm so sick of losing people," she sobbed into Julian's shoulder. "I'm so sick of losing people." After a moment, she let go of Julian's embrace and stormed off into the bathroom.

Julian tapped on the door and Mackenzie turned around to let him in. "Julian, I'm okay, but I'm ready to leave. I don't want to go to another funeral. I'm tired of this shit."

"Baby, I understand. We can leave tomorrow."

"NO. I want to leave now. I'm ready to start our life together. I want to leave now, Julian."

"Okay. Calm down, baby. I'll tell your folks, and we can catch a cab back to the airport. I have quite a bit of frequent flyer points that we can use for next to nothing. We can head to San Francisco from here. I'll call Ken back, and we can stay at a hotel and begin house hunting tomorrow."

"Good, because I refuse to attend another funeral." Mackenzie's voice was sharp and a bit harsh. She opened up the door and faced Lauren, Erica, and Aaron, who had emerged from his room in the back.

"We're leaving," she stated abruptly. "I'll call when we get settled in San Fran."

Without looking back at her family, or even hugging her niece and nephew, she opened the front door and headed out, with Julian following her with their luggage.

"Mackenzie, you can't keep running every time somebody dies," Lauren called out, as Mackenzie stomped down the rickety steps, unwilling to listen to reason.

Outside, in the still air, Julian called out to Mackenzie and petitioned her to wait so that they could catch a cab. She stopped and waited for Julian.

"Honey, come on, don't be ridiculous. We are in the heart of Brooklyn. You can't go taking off by yourself."

"Julian, I know I've been gone for a while, but I know these people here. And no matter what my status is now, we are one and the same."

Those words were somewhat of a shock to Julian because he didn't know how to take them. What exactly was his wife saying to him?

Chapter Five

Finally, after much turmoil, anxiety, and frustration, they arrived in San Francisco. The airport was as busy as New Year's Eve in Times Square. Even after a national disaster, people were coming and going as if what had taken place had nothing to do with them.

Men were in business suits and had laptops; women were in high fashion and strolled through as if they were on a photo shoot. There were also families that were leaving for vacations, which was just what Mackenzie needed to see. She used this to help her forget all about New York and Sam. She was ready to jump into high profile living.

"Well, if it isn't Ms. Mackenzie. Or should I say Mrs. Mackenzie?" Ken's deep voice called out.

"Hey, partner, how's it going?" Julian smiled back at Ken and extended his hand for a firm handshake.

"Waiting on you. The phones have been blowing up. I had to go ahead and hire another secretary. She's good—very sharp. You should approve."

Mackenzie waited until the business discourse ended, then smiled at Ken and gave him a warm hug. "Hey stranger. How are you?" she said.

"I'm good now. How are you, Mackenzie? Everything okay back home?"

"Yeah. Everything's okay. So, where's your wife? And when are we going to meet her?"

"Oh, you will. She went to the gym and had some other errands. Dinner tonight? I know you guys don't want to eat out after all that you've been through. In fact, you guys can stay with Ginger and I until you find something."

"Thanks man, but we really don't want to impose. A friend of mine already has a couple of homes for us to check out tomorrow. And if Mrs. Taylor finds anyone that she likes, we'll be moving in by week's end." Julian smiled and reached for Mackenzie's hand, kissing it.

"Okay, well, if you guys change your mind, just let us know. The offer won't change. Let's get the luggage and get you guys settled in. I know a real good hotel. All you have to do is wake up—everything else, they handle."

Julian looked strangely at Ken for a moment; it was as if Ken was telling on himself and forgot that Mackenzie was around.

But Mackenzie, who was anxious to go house hunting and get settled, didn't even pay attention to their male jargon.

They shuffled through the airport with its many faces, picked up their luggage successfully, and left to find a rental car company.

"This place is beautiful. I can't wait to get settled."

"Yes it is." Ken smiled back at Mackenzie. "The only problem may be the traffic, which is to be expected in a busy city. But the nightlife is awesome; there is always something to do."

"Yeah well, that's good to know, but I'm anxious to get to work. You guys can have the night life," Julian said.

"We'll have to get out at least once, honey. Please don't become some workaholic—then I'll be forced to go out alone. And you know I hate that."

"Oh that's fine, Mackenzie, let him. I'll take you out. Ginger doesn't like to get out much either. We can leave those two at home," Ken said, with a slight grin.

"Well thanks, partner, but I think I can handle my wife and her needs."

"Okay, well let's make a move."

"We're following you, right Ken?"

"Yep. I'll drive you guys to your rental, then, we can head out."

"Cool. Mackenzie, you want to drive so you can become familiar with the highways?"

"Yeah. Thanks honey. You are so sweet." Mackenzie smiled at Julian and winked.

"Okay, you love birds, let's make a move."

"Oh, come on, partner—don't get green face cause Ginger's not here," Julian said in a joking manner. But it caught Ken off guard.

"What do you mean, Julian?" Ken asked, in a slightly agitated tone.

"Well, you said she doesn't like to get out much, you know."

"No, I don't know."

"Hey man. It was just a joke. Lighten up. It's not that serious."

The moment was suddenly tense as Julian chartered on waters unknown. Mackenzie knew that the Ken she knew never showed any emotion or vulnerability, but at this moment, he was showing a side that was unlike him.

"Okay boys, there is much to do here in San Fran—I have to find a home, get prettied up, and take the bar, so let's go.

"Ken, do you know where we need to go to get set up for the exam?" Mackenzie asked, snapping Ken out of his moment of vulnerability.

"Yeah, my bad, Julian. Just a little tired, you know, getting everything set up until you guys made it here. I'm sorry that I snapped. I'm glad you guys are here, and we're doing this project together."

"It's cool, Ken. I'm glad we're doing this, too."

"Okay. Now that you guys are cool again, let's get out of this airport. I feel so gritty and dirty," Mackenzie said. She led the way, as if she knew where she was going. And they followed, as if she knew the way, too.

They picked up the car—a black, S-type Jaguar—Julian and Mackenzie loaded up, and then they proceeded to follow Ken to their hotel.

"Honey, do you think Ken is okay?" Mackenzie asked.

"I hope so. I just want to do my thing here with this firm. I don't want to deal with the other personal stuff."

"I thought Ken was your friend?"

"He is, somewhat. I know him from the law circle back in Dallas. I mean, he's not my best friend, but as far as business and law is concerned, he's good."

"So you trust him, right?"

"Yeah, I trust him with the business; otherwise, I wouldn't have done it. This is a big step. You know him, too, Mackenzie. Don't you?"

"Well yeah, through Nick and Tiph, but it's not like we have this history."

"Did you guys used to date?"

Mackenzie had forgotten that she'd never told Julian about the one date she'd had with Ken and the kiss they'd shared so many summers ago.

"No honey, we didn't date, we just went out once."

"Is that when I saw you guys after the wedding?"

"No, that was ages ago. I wasn't even twenty-one yet."

"Really? So, you think he still has the hots for you?"

"The hots? Honey, no. Ken's married, and even if he wasn't, it takes two. I could not be active in that because I'm happily married," Mackenzie said to Julian, as they looked each other in the eye.

"So, you're going to take the bar, too?"

"Yeah. I thought we both were. Right?"

"Well, I guess, but you know you don't have to work here. You can stay home or shop all day."

"Julian, that would drive me crazy. I want to get back into the courtroom and stare some prosecutor down with intimidation."

"Mackenzie, you don't have to work, baby; this firm will handle everything."

"Julian, I want to work. I'm not a stay-home type of woman. I will lose my mind at home. What would I do all day?"

"Cook, clean. Well, not clean, we'll have a maid for that."

"Did you just say, 'cook?' You're kidding, right?"

"Yeah, you know I am. Well, if you must, then I guess we'll both be practicing law here. Wait, why don't you work with Ken and I? We can use you, I'm sure."

"Oh, you know that would be too much testosterone for me. Baby, maybe I *will* stay home." The two laughed and continued to follow Ken down the highway.

Chapter Six

"Honey, I like it. This is the one."

"Are you sure? He said he has a couple more for us to look at."

"This is it, Julian. I want this one."

"Okay, I'll call him and let him know."

The two-story, stucco home with floor-length glass windows and palm trees was just what Mackenzie envisioned as home. It had five bedrooms, a breakfast nook, formal dining, huge living area, 3.5 bathrooms, and an outdoor pool shaped like a peanut. Not to mention the kitchen area which was huge, with an island and marble floors that were immaculate.

Julian was happy to oblige his wife's wishes and phoned the seller to tell him to draw up the necessary papers. It had only been the first day and the second house that they'd looked at, but Mackenzie was sure that this was the one. In her mind, she began to furnish it and make preparations for making it into a home.

"It's done. He said he could meet us here in about two hours with everything. Let's grab some lunch; he should be here by the time we get back."

"Great, because there is so much we have to do. My stuff in Atlanta will be here by Monday, the car by Tuesday. Did you decide about your things back in Dallas?"

"Yeah, once we get this all set, I'm going to fly back and wrap things up and drive back."

"Really? When did you decide that? That's a long trip, honey—a full day. You'll be tired."

"Yeah, I know. I guess I could have it shipped like you did, makes sense. Then at least I can get to work."

"I think that would be better. I'll miss you if you drive—that's so time consuming," Mackenzie told him, as they walked out to their rental.

"Yeah, and Ken said the bar will be given this Saturday morning. I can't afford to miss it. The next one isn't for another three months. I can't wait that long and expect Ken to do all of the work at the firm. They even let me do an emergency registration so I can't pass this opportunity up."

"That's true. I'll be busy getting this place decorated. Are you having your bedroom set here, or are we going to buy a new one?"

"Well, do you want a new set?" he asked.

"No, I think we can keep your bedroom set and save that money for Jay-Jay—maybe for furnishing her bedroom, or maybe the pool area."

"Okay, well I'll let you do the decorating; your place in Atlanta was really nice."

"Aww, thanks sweetie, but it was terribly lonely there without you."

"I knew you missed me, trying to act hard when I finally showed up."

"You almost believed it."

"No, I didn't. Once we slept together, I knew I had you back."

Mackenzie rolled her eyes playfully and got into the car.

"Honey, don't forget to call Ken about dinner tonight. Do they want to meet at their house or out somewhere? And is she going to be there this time? I can't believe they cancelled last night at the last minute because she'd made other plans."

"I know, I thought that was strange, too. You think she's cheating on Ken?"

"I don't know. I've never met her. I just know that they were married shortly after Nick and Tiph, and I guess a little before we were. I hope not. Ken is really nice."

"Yeah, no man deserves that."

"Or vice versa."

"Of course. Well, you know I'm a one woman man and with my soul mate, the woman of my dreams, my home girl, my partner for life."

"Oh, you're just saying that 'cause I'm here. But you know better. I'll leave so quick, you wouldn't even be able to blink."

"Baby, I would never cheat on you. You are everything I ever wanted in a woman. Nothing would ever make me leave you. Nothing."

"Nothing would ever make me leave you either."

They shared another mushy moment and then drove down to Quiznos for sandwiches. The warm, still air put them both in the mood for light sandwiches as opposed to something hot and heavy.

In between bites, they canoodled, laughed, and made plans to check out the beach, go shopping together (something they both enjoyed doing), as well as gather information about pool maintenance.

It was Wednesday, and Julian didn't have to go to the office until Monday. Ken told him that it would be better to just get his personal things straight, then start work on a Monday and be fresh and ready.

Not to mention he had to take the bar first before he could do anything. He was already licensed in Texas, so he would be covered until his results came in. If he failed, which was unlikely, he would have to stop practicing until he passed.

By the time they made it back to their new home, the owner was there, marking down things that he would fix before they moved in. From the front yard to the pool area, he took notes and assured Julian and Mackenzie that prior to them moving in, which could be as soon as Friday, he would have everything done.

They all agreed and signed the necessary paperwork and scheduled the tentative closing in approximately two weeks. The owner left and assured them once again that his workers would be there first thing in the morning to start the work.

Julian and Mackenzie, happy about purchasing their first home together, did what any couple would do—they christened it, in every room.

"Come here, *sexy gurrrl*," he said, pulling her into his erection and gripping her behind. They undressed quickly, and standing naked, Julian picked her up and carried her up into what would soon be their bedroom.

He tasted her in each room, savoring her taste, her smell, as she climaxed over and over again. Roughly, they sexed on the kitchen sink, making their own movie, gyrating as he went in from behind, quickly exploding on her back.

Just as they were getting dressed, the doorbell rang. "Who the heck could that be?" Mackenzie asked.

"I don't know. Maybe some salesman or solicitor"

Mackenzie shrugged as she fastened her lace bra and put her top back on.

Struggling to pull up his pants and find his shirt, Julian walked to the door to see who was knocking.

He opened the door and let out a familiar laugh, and their guest did the same.

Coming from the back of the house and retying her hair, Mackenzie was greeted by Ken.

"Hello, neighbor." He laughed like he knew what he'd interrupted.

"Hey Ken. How are you?"

"I'm good. Just came home to pick up some papers when I saw the rental that we'd picked up. I wanted to see if it was you all. We live right across the street."

"Really, in that big house I was telling Julian that I wished that one was for sale."

"Yep, that's our home. This is not too bad either. In fact, the only reason why we didn't get this one was because some other couple was looking at it, and they were pretty sure they were going to get it, but I guess it fell through."

"Wow, well no offense, but I'm glad. I love this place."

"Hey, we'll call you guys about dinner tonight," Julian said. "Didn't know if we were still on."

"No, it's good. Ginger and I just got our wires crossed last night. Tonight at our place around seven would be great."

Julian and Mackenzie looked at each other, and as if on cue then, both said, "Okay."

"So, when do you guys move in?"

"Two weeks from Friday! Can you believe that?"

"Oh yeah, they don't mess around. They will have this place spic and span by then," Ken said, looking the place over.

"Well, that's good to know."

"Look, I'll let you two finish up here, and we'll see you guys around seven. The house number is 706 Buena Vista."

They said their good byes until later, and Julian and Mackenzie went back to their hotel room to nap and freshen up.

They awoke around five thirty and began to get ready for dinner.

"Julian, what do you think she's like? This *Ginger* character."

"Honey, I don't know. I just hope there is no drama or mess tonight. She just seems so mysterious, like you don't know what to expect. I'm nervous."

"Really?" Mackenzie asked, letting out a short laugh. "Why?"

"I don't know. She's got Ken all on edge and I don't want to say anything that will set him or her off, especially her."

"I'm not nervous, but I am slightly intrigued by her and who she is. But you're right, she's a mystery."

"Well, she won't be after tonight, because I'm going to dissect her into pieces. Before we make it home, I'll tell you everything about her. Just wait and see."

"Okay, Sherlock, or should I say Matlock?" Mackenzie teased.

"So, what are we wearing? You know we only have honeymoon clothes."

"Yeah, I forgot about that. Well, it's just Ken and Mrs. Mysterious," Mackenzie jokingly stated. "Don't we have some jeans packed?"

"Yeah we do, that way we can really get on her nerves if she's prissy," Julian interjected, raising an eyebrow for added emphasis.

"You're so bad sometimes, Julian. But I feel like jeans anyway, so let's do it."

They dressed in their jeans, sandals, and summer tops and drove to Ken and Ginger's, admiring the comfort of the cool evening weather. The wind was blowing slightly, causing chills to cover Mackenzie's arms.

Julian, who had already taken to San Francisco's nighttime cool air, held her hand after rubbing her goose bumps. And in between smooches and laughs, the two made their way to the two-story, stucco home that was nestled within fine greenery and two palm trees.

They rang the doorbell in between more kisses and were caught off guard when the door gently opened, revealing the most beautiful creature either of them had ever seen.

Part II:

Mrs. Mysterious

Chapter Seven

At six feet, the beautiful, honey-brown and cinnamon woman, with curves in all the right places, had a smile that whispered, *come here* and eyelashes that curled just a bit, adding emphasis to her request. She had that Smokey, sultry Nona Gaye look.

Dressed in a sleeveless black dress that fit her figure, but was not too revealing, and sandals, her face was radiant, with everything perfectly placed. Even her shiny, jet-black hair, which was pulled up in a bun, was elegantly placed.

"Hello. You must be Mackenzie and Julian. It's a pleasure to finally meet you. I'm Ginger." Her disposition was warm and southern—definitely not rude or pretentious, as Mackenzie and Julian had thought.

"You guys come on in; Ken's out back on the grill," she added, allowing her guests in with a sheepish grin that caused Julian to feel slightly awkward.

Julian squeezed the hand of Mackenzie, who was as awestruck as he, but she managed to speak first.

"It's nice to meet you, Ginger, and we certainly thank you and Ken for having us over tonight," Mackenzie responded, smiling.

"Well, come on in and make yourselves at home. Dinner should be ready soon. Would you guys like something to drink? We have just about anything. Personally, I'm a wine drinker, but we can accommodate anything."

"We'll both have white wine," Mackenzie replied, as they followed

Ginger down a long hallway with ceramic print tiles and modern art that covered the walls. Everything was bright and full of color. The couch was a bright red, with modern, abstract chairs on each side and silver, odd-shaped tables.

"This is nice, Ginger," Mackenzie said, nodding at Ginger's taste in furniture.

"Well thank you, Ms. Mackenzie."

Her southern drawl was now obvious, which explained to Mackenzie why she was so friendly. It was all too familiar to Mackenzie how southerners always overdid themselves when being courteous. To her it was a strong indication that they were acting fake. She laughed to herself as she watched Ginger sashay through their lovely home.

"Ginger, can you tell me where the restroom is? Please, ma'am," Julian asked, sounding a bit nervous.

"Oh Julian, please, call me Ginger—no need for the word ma'am. My mother lives in Texas," she said, with a slight laugh.

Julian and Mackenzie laughed too.

"Glad to see you guys made it," Ken said, as he came in from the patio wearing a chef's hat and holding cooking utensils. He wore a smile that signaled he was happy today, and he was indeed in good company.

"Come on out back; the steaks should be done shortly."

"Well, you two go ahead, dear. I'm going to show Julian where the restroom is."

"Oh, okay. Well come on, Mackenzie, follow me," Ken said.

The four of them split into pairs and went into different directions of the house.

"So, Mackenzie, how do you like San Fran?" Ken asked, as they walked to the patio area "You guys are going to love it, I'm telling you. This place is awesome. And the firm is going to do real well. There is a great deal of money here. A lot of our clients will expect us to work discretely with their cases; given the nature and their status. We are going to make a killing."

"Really? I don't understand. What nature are we speaking of? And what type of clients are you guys going to represent?" She asked inquisitively.

"Well, you know, celebrities in the sports and entertainment industry who live alternatively and have gotten caught or who are being blackmailed by some of their former partners or bed fellows," Ken said in a sly tone.

"Huh, do you mean gay people that are part of the industry?"

"Precisely," Ken stated. "This is where the money is. There are tons of celebrities and sports figures that are in the closet, out of the closet, and doing scandalous things. They just expect not to get caught. That's where we come in."

"Julian knows about this? He didn't say anything to me about this."

"Yeah, he knows. We both decided to target that group in this location because so many of them migrate here or own property here. Most of it was his idea, to be honest. He didn't tell you?"

Mackenzie tried not to show her concern and shook her head at Ken's question, but in the back of her mind, she wondered about her husband's motives and why he hadn't told her about the nature of their firm. And more so, why would he ask her to work there?

Smallwood & Taylor—the gay friendly firm, she thought to herself, becoming infuriated.

"Mackenzie, are you all right? You seem to have drifted off."

"Oh no, I'm fine. Where is your restroom, Ken?"

"Umm, just down the hallway opposite the way you guys came in."

"Excuse me please, I'll be right back."

Mackenzie walked through the hallway trying not to show her disgust with Julian, but her blood was boiling, and she knew it would take everything in the world not to let her tongue loose on Julian in front of Ken and Ginger.

Caught up in her own emotions and filled with anger, Mackenzie unknowingly walked into a conversation between Julian and Ginger standing in the slightly darkened hallway by the bathroom.

"I swear I know you from somewhere. Are you sure you're not from

Oklahoma?"

"I'm pretty sure, Mr. Julian. Last I checked, I was born and raised in a small town right outside of Lubbock, Texas. I'm an only child. Sorry, it's not me."

They both laughed, not realizing Mackenzie had walked up.

"Oh, hey baby, what's up?" Julian said, noticing her at last.

"Nothing. I need to use the restroom. Excuse me." Mackenzie walked past Julian and Ginger without making eye contact and shut the door behind her.

Tapping on the plexi-glass door, Julian called out, "Honey, everything all right?"

"Well, I'll let you two talk." Ginger gave Julian a familiar smile and exited down the hallway, as Julian attentively watched.

"Julian, I'm fine; I just need to use the restroom. Is that okay?" Mackenzie said, as Julian turned his attention back to his wife.

"Well, sure honey, you just seemed a bit annoyed, that's all. Are you sure everything is okay?"

Not able to hold in her anger, Mackenzie pulled back the door and stared at Julian. "I said I was fine," she said angrily. "Don't ask that question again."

She proceeded to walk off, but Julian grabbed her by the arm. "Wait a minute. There *is* something wrong. It's not what you think. She just looks familiar, and we were talking about that. That's all. I promise."

"Please, don't flatter yourself. I could care less about you and Ginger. My problem is why didn't you tell me about the nature of the firm and what kind of clients you guys were going to represent? I thought you promised that you would give up that type of clientele."

Julian sighed, knowing that he'd messed up. "I was going to tell you. I was just waiting for the right time."

"Really? And when would that be? When I decided to work with you and Ken or when someone stumbles on my past and throws it in both our faces?"

"That's not going to happen. These people are not sport figures, they're entertainers. They would never make the connection."

"Well, I'm glad you're so sure."

"Come on, hon, it won't be that bad. That incident with that football player was rare. You have to admit that. And besides, this is California. You never had any female friends from here. Right?"

"What? Please tell me you didn't just ask that? I've never discussed that with you, and that's not the point. You lied to me, Julian. That's the problem."

"Well, I knew you would over-react and probably not want to work there. You have the experience; I just thought you would feel different once we arrived here."

"You thought wrong, Julian. And if you're referring to the firm in Atlanta, I left as soon as I found out about their charade. What is it about gay people that has you so fascinated? Why can't you work for other minorities and help them out?"

"Hon, you know there's no money there. This is where the money is."

"I'm glad I see what's most important to you."

Julian looked away then replied, "Listen this isn't that serious."

"Glad you think so," Mackenzie said, as she stormed off, leaving Julian standing in the hallway, massaging his temples.

The rest of the evening was spent with the two couples getting to know one another, playing charades and sipping on expensive wine that Ken and Ginger swore by. Mackenzie pretended as best as she could, wanting desperately to hide her level of discomfort. But she knew Julian's association with people in the lifestyle whether it be prominent folk or everyday people only meant one thing for her--trouble or drama!

Chapter Eight

"Are you coming to bed?"

"No, I have some things to work on. I'll probably just sleep out here." Mackenzie said curtly.

"Are you sure? I could use the company."

"Yes, I'm sure. Good night."

Julian stared at the back of his wife's head as she continued to work on the couch reading case studies. She knew he was watching, but she refused to look back.

As he walked off, Mackenzie put down her pen and papers and surveyed the room. The newly decorated home didn't feel like much of a home to her anymore. All of her excitement had turned into disappointment, and she wondered if she could ever forgive Julian for not telling her about the firm.

It had almost been a month, and the two barely talked, and when she did sleep in the bedroom, she made sure she was fast asleep before Julian arrived. Any advances that he attempted were also shot down, with excuses of having a headache or Mackenzie simply not being in the mood.

She missed the grand opening of the firm and passed on just about all of the special events that Julian had attended.

In between dodging him, she spent most of her time driving along the coast, sitting in coffees shops, or online. This was definitely not what she had planned on as her new life in San Francisco. But she didn't want to be *fake* and go to flashy parties with entertainers that were leading double lives and using her husband to cover for them or make some deal under the table so she could live a life of luxury.

She simply refused to play the role and decided that she would not be attending any functions or associating herself with her husband's firm. She just couldn't.

"Mackenzie."

Mackenzie sighed trying to let Julian know that she still wasn't in the mood to talk or do anything that involved him.

"Yes, Julian?" she replied, sounding slightly agitated. "And no, I still don't want a maid around here."

"It's the telephone, sweetie."

Mackenzie turned around, puzzled, because she had no friends, had cut off her family again, so for the life of her she had no idea who would be calling her at nine in the evening.

"Who is it?"

"Pickup and find out."

Mackenzie shot him a go to hell look and proceeded to get up off the couch. With her hair hanging down her back and dressed in hospital scrubs, she walked into the kitchen and flipped on the light before reaching for the receiver. "Hello?"

"Hey, girl."

"Hello, who is this?" Mackenzie asked, trying not to sound too rude.

"It's Ginger."

"Oh, I'm sorry, I didn't catch the voice," Mackenzie replied, sounding sarcastic because she and Ginger both knew that they hadn't talked since the night of the dinner at her house. Mackenzie had been stand offish then, so *why all of a sudden pretend now?* She thought to herself.

"So, how have you been?"

"Just fine, and you?"

"I'm doing fine, missed you at a couple of the functions though."

"Yeah, I've been busy."

"Really? Doing what?"

"Excuse me?"

"No, I was just wondering what you've been up to; and, I thought maybe we could meet up for cappuccino or something."

"Well, I doubt that. I really don't have the time."

"You are tough. I thought that was a rumor about people from New York."

"Well, I've been in Texas for most of my adult life, and I'm not being rude, just honest," Mackenzie said, attempting to upset Ginger in hopes that she would end the unwanted phone call.

"And you take the term 'bitch' to another level, might I add."

"Well, I've been told that I have that effect at times—without trying, might I add."

"And a cocky bitch at that."

"And if you call me bitch one more time, I'm going to reach through this phone and slap the shit out of you."

"No offense, but I would be on the other line phoning Maury, Oprah, Sally, The Enquirer, the British Tabloids, and whoever else I could possibly sell my story to. I would even offer my own byline: **MISERABLE HOUSEWIFE SNAPS AND REACHES THROUGH PHONE TO SLAP NEIGHBOR**. Girl, I would make a ton of money," Ginger said, as the two of them started laughing.

"Ginger, you're crazy. What do you want anyway? Didn't my husband tell you I wasn't being too verbal these days?"

"Actually, I've called several times, and we've talked, but the only thing he's said was that you were trying to adjust and to just give you some time."

Mackenzie pulled the phone away from her mouth to yawn before responding.

"Oh yeah, well I guess."

"So, what ARE you doing, girl?"

"Girl, nothing—needing a break, that's all."

"Really? From what? You haven't done anything since you've been here," she said, with a chuckle.

"And why are you paying attention to me and what I'm doing?"

"Well, it's not too hard considering the fact that our husbands are partners and we're neighbors. Information like that just comes naturally," Ginger replied, enjoying the exchange of verbal warfare.

"So, how's Ken? Are you driving him crazy over there?"

"Wouldn't you like to know?"

"Actually, I could care less. But, I figured I would ask and keep up this charade out of sympathy for you. It's obvious you are in need of a friend, Ms. Ginger."

"Ms. Mackenzie is that a proposition for a friendship?"

"Not really" Mackenzie replied startled at Gingers' response. *Does she really think we can just become friends that easy?*

"So, what are you doing tomorrow? Do you want to get out, maybe go down to the mall or have lunch?"

"I have to check my calendar; I've been quite busy these days, you know."

"Oh yeah, I know. Bye girl. Just call me if you change your mind."

"I will. You have a good night, and thanks for calling."

Mackenzie shook her head out of disbelief and laughed as she thought about the conversation she'd just had with Ginger. She chuckled at Gingers assertiveness.

"Did you say something, hon?"

"No Julian, I didn't," she said, standing to put up the phone and ignoring Julian's presence.

She entered the kitchen to hang up the cordless phone and checked the fridge for some cut up cantaloupe.

"I'm sorry I didn't tell you about the firm. I wasn't trying to hide anything from you."

Mackenzie ignored Julian and his words and proceeded to fix a sandwich, placing the ingredients on the island in the center of the kitchen. She placed each item, the turkey, white cheddar cheese, lettuce, tomatoes, and hoagie bread neatly on the counter, still ignoring him.

"You can't continue to ignore me. I have needs. I didn't marry you to go through this. We should have resolved this by now. I don't know how much more of this I can take."

She fixed her sandwich, and searched for Doritos to accompany her sandwich. Mackenzie continued to ignore Julian, who was now visibly upset.

"Is this about you? Is that why you're upset? When are you going to let go of your past and stop waiting for it to explode in your face? Mackenzie, if you're so over it, why do you get so upset when any aspect of that lifestyle is brought up? Did you ever stop to think that maybe I didn't tell you because I didn't know how you would react? And now that I see, I'm glad I didn't."

She stared back at Julian and held back her tears. His harsh words were painful, causing her to feel a sense of betrayal. And without hesitation, she walked off, leaving her dinner and Julian just as they were in the kitchen.

Chapter Nine

Even the comfort, coziness, and compact space of her Z3 wasn't enough to shelter Mackenzie from her feelings of abandonment and betrayal. *How could Julian say those harsh words to her she wondered?*

Up and down the numerous hills and cluttered streets, Mackenzie thought long and hard about her life and how things were not turning out as she'd planned. Her marriage certainly wasn't, not to mention her non-existent career. For the last month, she had moped around mad at her husband and the world because he'd decided to start a firm that represented entertainers who led alternative lifestyles. And he couldn't understand why it bothered her.

It scared her; him working so close to her past. In the back of her mind, she always felt something would come back to haunt her.

Just the thought of it made her furious all over again. So much so that she had to stop her roadster and get a grip before she flipped it over going up and down the hills.

Coming to a complete stop, she turned off her car and ran her fingers through her long hair; unloosening her scrunchy.

"God, I hate him," she moaned to herself, as she turned up the street searching for a place to park. The streets of San Francisco were quiet, with a mild northern wind blowing slightly. She searched for her cell phone; which was tucked safely in the glove compartment. Mackenzie cleared her throat as she dialed information.

"Yes, can I have the listing for Kenneth Smallwood or Ginger Smallwood?"

"One moment please. Is that in the bay area?"

"Yes, ma'am it is."

"We have two listings. The listing for Ginger Smallwood is unlisted. Would you like the listing for Kenneth Smallwood?"

"Yes, that would be fine."

"Please hold for the number."

Mackenzie scurried for a pen and wrote down the number on a napkin that was in her passenger seat. She lifted up, re-adjusting her hospital pants; which were sticking to her black leather seats, then dialed the number.

"Yes, may I speak with Ginger Smallwood?"

"This is Ginger, whose calling?"

"Hey Ginger, it's me, Mackenzie. Are you busy?"

"Not at all is everything okay?"

"Not really. Can you talk?"

"Sure. Where are you?"

"I don't even know some street, probably a little south of downtown. Are you familiar with downtown?"

"Yep, I don't work too far from there. There's a coffee shop on the south side on Oak St. It's very quaint a lot of the doctors from the hospital go there after, or in between shifts. We can meet there. Have you passed the hospital yet?"

"It's real big, right?"

"Yes, it's the only one down there. The coffee shop is adjacent to the hospital. You can't miss it."

"Okay, if I get lost, I'll call you back."

"Okay, but you're not too far. I'll see you in about fifteen minutes?"

Mackenzie turned the steering wheel and made a u-turn in the middle of the street only to be greeted by horns and flashing lights. The street was a one-way. She had to stop and reverse, and then turn back around.

After a couple of turns and reading street signs, she found the tiny coffee shop that was barely lit, with bistro tables and black and white photos of nameless faces. Some were of adults, some children, and some of puppies, kittens, or matured dogs and cats.

It was a typical café with a long counter filled with sugar dispensers, crème, and napkins.

The young, hippie, white guy with long hair and the even younger waitress with golden ringlets that fell shy of her jaw bone stood side by side, waiting on some family members of patients at the hospital. The place was filled with doctors that were despondent after losing patients and doctors in between calls, all in need of a late night fix of caffeine. And then there were also those who simply needed a refuge for the night—a place to hide, a place to seek friendly fire.

Mackenzie surveyed the café, looking for Ginger in hopes that she could let out her woes. She didn't even mind the fact that she and Ginger weren't friends. But since falling out with her sisters and not being close to her aunt Cecile back in Texas anymore, she knew Ginger would have to suffice tonight.

Mackenzie found a window table and sat facing the door, then adjusted her hospital pants and retied her hair.

She couldn't help but let her mind drift back to Julian and his hurtful words. It was as if it was a scratched record, and over and over again she heard, *"If you're so over it, why do you get so upset anytime any aspect of that lifestyle is brought up?"*

Mackenzie clenched her fist at the thought of Julian and his words. In her heart, she believed he of all people should understand after the ordeal with Jay-Jay and Erasmus. "Guess he lied about that, too," she mumbled to herself, as the white, male waiter walked to her table.

"Are you going to enjoy any of our wonderful coffee today, sister?" The awkwardness of his tone caught Mackenzie off guard, causing her to take a double look.

"Do you have the hazelnut cappuccino? And if so, can you mix it with French vanilla? I'll have a large cup if you have it."

"Yes, ma'am, we do. Coming right up."

"Hey Mackenzie," Ginger said, as the waiter walked off.

"Hey, Ms. Ginger, thanks for coming." Mackenzie tried not to sound unappreciative.

Ginger took her seat across from Mackenzie as the two began to adjust.

"I'm not keeping you from anything, am I?" Mackenzie asked, hoping that Ginger had plenty of time to spare.

"Not at all, dear. I have a meeting at noon tomorrow for a couple of hours, and then I'm off for the rest of the day. She smiled—the red velour warm-up made her smile radiant.

"So, what is it that you do again, Ginger?"

"I'm a Pediatrician."

"Wow, I bet you really enjoy your job. I wish I was working. I miss the courtroom and all the things that go on. It's so interesting."

"So, why don't you practice here? Take the bar. Trust me, you can find a job easily. Julian said you have a strong background, and was top in your class. He even said you skipped grad school and went to law school straight from undergrad, that's pretty impressive."

Mackenzie rolled her eyes. "Yeah, well whatever. That's another story that makes me want to puke right now."

"Did I say something wrong, Mackenzie?"

"No. I just don't want to hear anything he has to say right now, that's all."

"Why? I thought you two were happy. I thought you wanted to be here?"

"Here you go, sister. And what can I get for you?" the waiter asked, all smiles interrupting their conversation.

Ginger smiled back. "I'll have the hazelnut capp with a little cinnamon. Large is fine."

"Okay, coming right up." He smiled and offered a flirtatious wink.

"So, you like hazelnut, too? I usually mix mine with french vanilla."

"Well, wait until we get a little fall weather. There are several other coffee shops I like to go to when I'm off. I'll have to take you sometime."

"Okay I've been dying during the summer with anticipation of fall coming so I can just sit and take in the season. And all the changes that occur."

"Okay, sounds like a plan, but I didn't think that San Francisco had a fall season. That's news to me. But I'm new here as well, so we'll see."

"Now, back to Julian I don't understand," Ginger asked inquisitively.

"It's complicated. Maybe one day I'll tell you."

"Must be pretty deep then I guess I can wait," Ginger said, attempting to extend a hand of friendship, which Mackenzie ignored. Her mind drifted back to Ginger and Julian's excursion of conversation when they'd first met Ginger.

"So, did you and Julian finally figure out where you know each other from?" Mackenzie asked curtly.

"Actually, he had me confused with someone else that he knew. I told him it wasn't me, and after he spent one day with tons of questions, he realized it was someone else. It was quite funny.

"Listen Mackenzie, I don't know what's going on. Ken hasn't said anything, and Julian and I don't talk either. I've called a few times for you, and he's politely told me that you were either busy or not home, which I kind of thought was odd because I would see your car there. Don't you drive the Z3, and he has the sedan?"

"Yeah," Mackenzie replied, trying not to sound rude.

"Well, anyway, you know they're having an event tomorrow night at one of the local restaurants to celebrate winning their first major case. Julian didn't tell you?"

"Maybe he did, I'm just not too big on his words these days."

"Mackenzie, I think you should come. Maybe it will help you get some peace."

"You think so? I don't know, Ginger. I haven't been out the house, my hair is a mess, I don't even think I have anything to wear."

"You don't have anything to wear? I find that hard to believe. You seem like a diva with a closet filled with clothes."

"Well, I have some things. Julian and I loved to shop when things were better. I guess I'll go, if I can, Ginger."

"You can," Ginger stated, as she sipped on the cappuccino that the waiter brought over. "I'm going to help you. We can go together. I presume the guys will go from work, since Ken told me to meet him there. We can ride together, or we can follow each other just in case you want to leave."

"But what about my hair? Well, I guess I could pull it back in a bun and wear one of my slinky black dresses. You think I should?"

"That's sounds good. See, you can go. We'll have fun, too. I promise."

Chapter Ten

God, I hope I'm not making a mistake going there tonight, Mackenzie thought to herself as she drove, trying to follow Ginger through the evening traffic that cluttered the San Francisco streets.

In between stops, Mackenzie checked her makeup, her hair, and looked over her black dress, which she'd bought earlier that morning at the Banana Republic.

She finally convinced herself that if she was going to go, she had to do it right, and that basically meant buying something new and getting a manicure and a pedicure.

It was a cool evening in the early fall of October, but the spaghetti-strapped dress and laced strap shoes were still a fashion statement. If it was one thing that Mackenzie prided herself in, it was dressing the part. She knew she had to set the tone, since she had been non-existent in her husband's business affairs.

She wanted Julian to see how beautiful she was and how women her age were either out of shape, overweight with kids, or bitter.

She knew she was bitter, but she also knew she had the body, the brains, and the drive that was just a turn-on for men that were professional and secure. Plainly put, she knew her outfit would drive her husband crazy and let the women that were probably hovering over her husband know who he came home to every night—even if they hadn't shared the same bed for over a month.

She approached the valet parking, as she trailed Ginger's black Range

Rover. Mackenzie took another deep breath, checked her hair and makeup, then stepped out as the young, Asian attendant with bad acne and a spiked haircut assisted her.

Cool and casual, the two women walked in procession to the Spanish restaurant in silence.

They reached the restaurant, *La La Linda*. Its exterior was colorful and inviting, with a touch of class. The hostess greeted them outside and showed them in.

The restaurant was filled with suits and ties and young women at their disposal. Ginger led the way, leaving Mackenzie to think about her decision to come and take in all the beauty that surrounded her and, to her surprise, her husband.

She let out a sigh and continued on as she approached Julian, who was standing closely to a young, Hispanic woman that was wiping off his face and flirting with him.

Part of Mackenzie wanted to turn around and leave while the other was curious to meet the woman that had her husband's undivided attention.

Ginger turned around to face Mackenzie and asked, "Sure you want to do this, kiddo?"

Mackenzie twisted her lip some and responded, "Yep."

"Hello, honey, how are you?" she asked a startled Julian.

"Mackenzie. Oh, hey hon."

His Hispanic friend, still not moving, looked at Mackenzie as if she'd interrupted something.

"Hello, I'm Mackenzie, Julian's wife, and you are?" she asked, extending her hand.

"Oh, I'm sorry. I'm his secretary. You know, at these functions I have to protect him from all of these beautiful women. If you know what I mean." She winked at Mackenzie. "I'm Anayelica Moreno. It's nice to finally meet you. I was starting to think that he wasn't married," she said, in a heavy Latin accent.

"Oh, he's still married, if you know what I mean," Mackenzie said sarcastically, returning Anayelica's wink.

"Can you excuse us for a moment, Ana?" she said, refusing to say her entire name.

"Sure, I'll be right over there." She pointed out a table filled with suits and martini glasses.

"Ginger, give me a sec."

"Okay, I'm going to find Ken and make sure Ms. Horowitz's old behind doesn't have him pinned up somewhere," she stated, rolling her eyes at Julian.

"Why didn't you tell me you were coming?"

"I didn't know I had to. Is there a problem?"

"No, but we could have come together instead of you showing up here with Ginger. But seems like she wanted it that way. Hope she's satisfied."

"What's that supposed to mean?"

"Nothing. You want something to drink?"

"No, are you going to introduce me to your co-workers?"

"I hadn't planned on it. Is that why you're here?"

"No, I just figured you would."

There was tension between the two of them, and it was hard to conceal. They had become complete strangers in less than two months after being married.

"I guess I'll leave you to your secretary and let her continue to protect you from the many beautiful women in the room. Let's see all one, two, three, four…seven, all seven of them."

"If that's what you want to do, Mackenzie."

She blew out hard and rolled her eyes at Julian. "Goodnight."

She zipped through the crowd, trying to find Ginger and Ken. Her patience was just about gone, and if she knew herself, she knew she had better leave before she caused a scene.

With no luck finding Ginger, she left the restaurant in hopes that she could just find her car and zoom home.

The nightly chill had set in, and Mackenzie thought about her outfit, which now seemed inappropriate.

"Mackenzie, are you ready to leave?" the familiar voice called from behind her.

"Yes, please, I've got to get as far away from here as possible," she said, as she paused to wait on Ginger.

"Come on, I have just the perfect place."

Mackenzie left her car and they drove quietly to an apartment building not too far from the hospital. It was a chic and artsy building.

"This is my home away from home. Come on in and make yourself at home. I have wine in the fridge, a couple of beers, and some of the hard stuff on the counter."

"I really need a drink."

"I'll tell you what, you go get comfortable, there's some sweats or scrubs in the back room, and I'll fix you something."

"Thanks, Ginger."

"Sure thing."

Mackenzie returned in oversized scrubs and an Alumni Tee from UT Austin and a pair of socks. She sat on the modern, bright red leather seat and sighed softly. She didn't know what to make of Julian and his new secretary. Her heart sank a little. She knew she had no patience for infidelity and with a blink she would divorce Julian and never look back.

To her, that was her one true flaw—she had no problems leaving without any explanation. If you backed her up against a wall, she would either strike hard or simply retreat. Her problem was she didn't know when to do which.

"You okay, Mackenzie?" Ginger asked, handing her a shot glass.

"I've been better."

"Well, take a shot of this."

"What is it?"

"It's a buttery nipple—you'll love it."

"Really? I've never heard of such a thing."

"Come on . . . you ready. On three."

"One . . . two . . . three." They put the glasses to their mouths and in one gulp, drank.

"Now that's strong," Mackenzie let out in a light whisper.

"Have another?"

"Sure, why not. He can't have all the fun tonight." Mackenzie smiled and watched as Ginger walked off to get a couple more buttery nipples.

They sat and drank a few more, followed by a couple of beers, and laughed while listening to the best of Ce Ce Peniston, both mouthing the words and shaking their heads to the lyrics of "Just Walk On."

"Do you smoke, Mackenzie?" Ginger asked, with smoky eyes and a schoolgirl grin.

"Cigarettes? Nah, they smell horrible to me."

"No, silly. I mean marijuana, weed, or like my West Indian friends say, *Ganja*," she said, as the word seemed to roll off of her tongue, simmering with intensity.

"Oh, definitely not."

"Do you mind if I have a little smoke?"

"No, not at all, this is your place—just crack the window a little." They both looked at each other and then let out a huge laugh.

"Well, maybe not, it *is* against the law," Mackenzie said.

"Only sometimes, but I don't feel like explaining that. Hang on—let me go get my stash."

The two shared another laugh as Ginger went to the back area and retrieved a baggie filled with tightly rolled joints. "Are you sure you don't want to try any?"

"I'm sure—knock yourself out. I still have to find a job. I can't afford to fail a drug test." The two laughed again.

"I may be getting a divorce," Mackenzie said, changing the tone of their conversation.

Ginger sat quietly and lit her joint and inhaled. Smoothly as she exhaled she replied, "Are you okay with that?"

"Doesn't look like I have a choice."

"Sure you do. You have plenty of choices," she sat Indian style and smiled.

"Ginger, you don't understand—better yet, if you only knew."

"Who wants to get a divorce after being married for only two months?"

"Maybe I do. You'd be surprised. Trust me, it's complicated."

"So, why don't you?"

"Why don't I what?"

"Trust me."

"I never said that I didn't."

"You didn't have to, Mackenzie; it's obvious that you don't trust anyone."

"Really, I thought I'd loosened up some."

"Nope, but it's isn't too late to start. You can start with us. That is, if you want to trust me."

"Ginger, it's not that—things are just complicated in my life."

"You want to talk about it?"

"You would never understand."

"Why don't you try me?"

Mackenzie was tempted to lay all of her burdens down on Ginger. She had wanted so much to be able to talk to someone about her past and why she was so mad at Julian. But her trust issues were another of her flaws that she wanted to believe didn't exist.

"Maybe some other time, Ginger. Besides, my eyelids are getting extremely heavy. Do you have an extra pillow?"

"Sure, you can lie on my shoulder." She motioned for Mackenzie to come closer.

"No thanks, but I'd better get going; it's getting late. Julian doesn't know where I am. He'll worry."

"He hasn't called has he?"

Mackenzie sadly responded, "No." Hours had already passed by but she didn't want to acknowledge this sooner. She missed the moments when Julian worried about her and the many times he called to check on her when she was late getting in from school or the library.

"Do you have anymore beers left?"

"Of course, have another?"

"Yeah. Hook a sister up."

"Only on one condition."

"What's that?" Mackenzie said, with a warm and friendly smile.

"You have to promise that you will stay here tonight and sleep off your alcohol," she said, standing over Mackenzie and pulling her up from the sofa, catching her in her arms.

"You promise?"

Mackenzie held on as the room spun around like a spin top and laughed. "I promise."

"Come on, follow me."

"Okay, but don't move so fast—my head is spinning remember?." She giggled.

"Give me your hand."

"Look at you, still sashaying like a true diva. You should have seen how everybody looked at you when we walked into that restaurant; it was like all eyes on you. You're so beautiful, Ginger."

Mackenzie reached out her hand as Ginger held it and led her into the darkened kitchen. But she did something Mackenzie wasn't expecting. She turned around in mid stride and pulled her close, grabbing Mackenzie's waist and she kissed her.

Mackenzie quickly pulled back and stared at Ginger, ignoring her wanting eyes. She pulled away from her embrace. "I've got to go." Suddenly, she felt sober again.

"But you promised."

"No, I'm okay," she said, backing away from Ginger. *Oh my Damn! She just kissed me!*

"Mackenzie. Come on, it'll be nice—it may be what you need." Ginger said with a smile; her teeth were as bright as the morning sun in her dark kitchen.

"Excuse me?"

"Mackenzie, wait. I thought I saw something earlier, that's all. I'm sorry."

"Saw what?" Mackenzie said with an attitude. *She has just propositioned me, what the fuck is this? The twilight zone? Here I am thinking she may be after my husband and it's me she wants to screw!*

"I was out of line. I'm sorry."

"Yeah, you were out of line. I'd better get going. Where's my keys?" Mackenzie asked, bothered by Ginger's sudden change in character. *Shit she wasn't even slick about it just 'wham' and her tongue is down my throat; ticklin' me and shit, rufflin' my damn feathers!*

"Right on the table." Ginger curtly said snapping Mackenzie out of her mental soliloquy.

Mackenzie grabbed her keys and left as fast as she could. She hadn't realized that she had no idea where her car was or the fact that she didn't even drive. Exasperated, she tried to gather her thoughts and figure out where she had parked. She reached for her cell phone in her tiny sequin purse but realized that she didn't have that either.

The downtown area was a ghost town, but Mackenzie managed to get a hold of herself, and located a pay phone. She called information and found a cab company. She told them where she was and prayed that they would come. Within five minutes, they arrived and delivered her safely to her home.

She let herself in and shut the door behind her. Julian hadn't made it home yet; she hadn't seen his car keys on the holder when she'd placed hers there. She sighed with disappointment.

Her mind went back to Ginger and all of the fun they'd had—until she'd crossed the line. Mackenzie felt bemused, yet enchanted with what she'd seen and felt.

She ignored her thoughts and began to prepare herself for a shower. She wondered where Julian could be, and how he could easily walk out on their marriage. Sifting through her armoire for something comfortable to wear, she caught a glimpse of Julian, fully clothed, lying in bed asleep with his cell phone and keys on his chest. His tie was off and his pressed shirt was slightly wrinkled, the make-up stains on his collar made her think of his pushy secretary. *I guess she didn't protect him all night!*

But she was glad that he had indeed come home. Mackenzie quietly walked over to him and placed her hand on his cell phone. She had to know if he was cheating on her. She pushed the button that said last number dialed and waited as the phone read back, "Wifey." Mackenzie continued to scroll down, checking the calls and the times, only to find that he had called her most of the evening—or his office. She smiled.

She placed his phone on his charger and took off his shoes, then placed his keys on the nightstand and helped him get comfortable. She ran her shower water and took off her clothes, attempting to bury the events that had taken place. She had to talk with Julian and clear her mind. She had to demolish any thoughts of Ginger while Julian slept.

Quickly, she showered and washed her hair. Mackenzie toweled up her hair and wrapped herself in a robe when she remembered that she was expecting an email from Nick and Tiphane.

She sat quietly at her desk and waited for the usual sound from AOL, then proceeded to check her mail. She had just hit the reply button to an old email that Tiphane had sent when her screen lit up.

KG1999 has sent you an instant message. Would you like to reply? : Mackenzie hit the yes button and waited for the message to pop up.

KG1999: I thought you would be sleeping.

Mackenzie&Julian: Who is this?

KG1999: Go to eyeball chat.com. It's at the bottom of your screen should be.

Mackenzie searched the bottom of her screen and saw the icon with a huge eye and clicked it twice.

The screen became a moving camera and Mackenzie looked closely, trying to see what was on her screen.

KG1999: Can you see me yet?

Mackenzie&Julian: Not really.

KG1999: Make your screen bigger by hitting the maximize button.

Mackenzie&Julian: Okay.

Mackenzie hit the maximize button and waited for her screen to adjust. Moments later, she was face to face with Ms. Ginger sitting at her computer in a cream-colored negligée.

KG1999: Are you there??

Mackenzie&Julian: Yes.

KG1999: Can you see me?

Mackenzie&Julian: Yes.

KG1999: Can you talk?

Mackenzie&Julian: Not really, about to go to bed.

KG1999: I really want to talk to you. I'm wondering what I should do??

Mackenzie&Julian: I'm really tired.

KG1999: Do you think we can do this again?? I enjoyed your company.

Mackenzie quickly signed off. Her heart was beating a mile a minute. She looked over at Julian and went to join him as he slept. And for the first time in a long time, she snuggled up beside him and allowed him to hold her as they slept peacefully, forgetting their own troubles.

Mental note-check Ginger's ass tomorrow about overstepping her boundaries!

Chapter Eleven

"Good morning." Julian spoke softly.

"Good morning."

"Would you like some breakfast? I fixed some french toast and a little coffee."

"Sure. I'm a little hungry," she said, as she walked into the bathroom to clean up.

After she washed her face, brushed her teeth, and pulled up her hair, she joined Julian in the breakfast nook.

"Here you are. There's fresh fruit also."

"All this for me?"

"Yep, you said you were hungry."

She smiled. "Thank you, Julian."

"You're welcome. Listen Mackenzie, I'm sorry about last night. I didn't think you would come if I asked you—then you showed up with Ginger. I didn't know what to think. I was being defensive."

"Yeah, it was her idea. I guess I wasn't expecting you to be there with anyone. Who is she?"

"Just our secretary. She's been with us for about a month now. She's the one Ken hired before we arrived here."

"It just looked like so much more."

"I know, and I apologize for that."

"Julian, we really need to talk."

"I know. I took the day off so we can spend some time together to talk. I know there's a lot we have to discuss and a lot of decisions we need to make."

Mackenzie nodded her head in agreement.

"As soon as we finish breakfast, I'll have a driver come to scoop us up, and we can get lost."

"Really? Where will we go?"

"I just figure we would drive down the coast and just talk."

"Wow, I'm excited. Have you eaten yet?"

"Yes, I'm going to shower and wait on you."

Mackenzie nodded her head as she ate her breakfast, then she quickly showered as he dressed. After her shower she put on some Capri shorts and a sleeveless turtleneck and sandals. The fall weather felt more like the first day of spring. It felt like a new beginning.

The driver arrived promptly and the two sat comfortably in the back of the car looking at one another. Julian was still as sexy as he had ever been to her. His glistening eyes and beautiful smile were radiant.

"Mackenzie, I was wrong to decide about this firm without telling you. I knew you wouldn't agree, but I wanted it so bad. Ken had no idea about your past. I hadn't told him until we made it here, when everything blew up in my face. I don't want to lose you over this. I told Ken that I would sell him my partnership, and you and I can start over.

"I'll do whatever you want me to do so we can fix this. I also have one of my friends looking into Jay-Jay and Erasmus. He said that we definitely would have a case and should be able to get her back soon."

"Julian wait, you should have told me about the firm and its arrangements, but I can't let you sell your half to please me. What about your dreams? I just wished I would have known initially. And you know why."

"I know, and I've wrestled with this for a while now. I handled it all wrong. Can you ever forgive me, sweetie?"

She smiled at Julian because she had missed him terribly and no longer wanted to fight. She wanted to make love to him right there and get lost in his eyes.

"Yes, I forgive you. I miss you so much, sweetie." She reached out to Julian, who quickly embraced her and kissed her passionately.

"I want to make love to you. I miss the taste of your body and how you feel in my arms." And like two high school sweethearts, they ignored the driver and allowed their desire to take control. They made love in the backseat as the driver turned up the radio, which was playing light jazz, and rolled back the moon-roof to include the light whistle of the wind.

Mackenzie slipped out of her Capris without embarrassment while Julian unfastened his pants. His erect penis popped out and stood at full attention.

"God, I missed you so much."

"I've missed you, too," she said, arching her back and moving up and down with the car swiftly moving. Julian always knew how to hit her spot, knowing that she loved being on top. He pushed in deep with full extension, gently rubbing against her clitoris. With seconds gone by, he jerked, and she jerked as warm sperm filled her insides.

"So what now?" she said, smiling and sliding off, reaching for her Capris.

"We need to make a trip back to Texas and meet with Jonathan and process the necessary paperwork. Then wait for a response," he said, catching his breath. "Damn, that was good." He smiled.

"Do you think they'll fight me?"

"I don't know. Erasmus seemed pretty cool when I met her. And wasn't she trying to get you to help her with Jay-Jay?"

"Yep, but I was so worried about telling you—that's why I lied. She always said I should have told you up front about everything."

"I know, but let's not worry about that now. We have to concentrate on getting Jay-Jay back. Whatever it takes."

"You sure you want to do this for me?"

"Baby, I want you to be happy. I know this has been hard for you, and we've wasted too much time already."

"So, when do we leave?" Mackenzie asked, brimming with excitement and fastening her pants while Julian did the same.

"I made reservations for next Friday at noon. We should arrive at Love Field at 3:15 that afternoon."

"Julian, this means so much to me. Thank you."

"Anything for you.

"Hey Sid, why don't you run us by a little bistro or something so we can get something to eat?"

"Sure thing, boss. Any place in particular?"

Julian looked at a starry-eyed Mackenzie to see if she had any suggestions.

"What about the soup and salad bar down by the mall?"

"Sure thing, Mrs. Taylor. We'll be there in about 15 minutes, tops."

They smiled and held each other while Sid zipped in and out of traffic to the soup and salad bar. The restaurant had become a favorite for Mackenzie during a lot of her free time. They ordered takeout and continued to tour around the city, enjoying each other's company.

They made it home late that evening, refreshed and with a renewed love. They were preparing for Jay-Jay to join them and talked about schooling for her and making additions to their home. They had even made plans to go to Toys R Us to pick up a child's necessities, like a bicycle, Play-station, and dolls.

"Oh hon, Ginger called while you were in the shower this morning. I just remembered to tell you when I saw the answering machine blinking."

"Did she say what she wanted?" Mackenzie asked, ignoring the sudden stomachache that ailed her.

"Well, she apologized to me for the other night, said she was just trying to help out and wanted to make sure that you were okay."

"Okay with what?"

"She didn't say, just said to tell you that she was concerned and to call when you get a chance, or stop by."

"Okay. I'll call when I get up in the morning."

"You know, you two should become friends. Ginger isn't that bad is she? And I probably shouldn't tell you this because it was supposed to be a surprise; Ken and I booked you two a weekend trip down in Miami Beach at the Eden Roc Resort for the weekend after next. How's that sound?"

"You did. Wow! But I'd rather go with you, hon. WE need a vacation."

"I know, but Ken and I figured you two would love all of the 'girly things' the two of you could do and then all of the shopping. I thought you would love the idea."

"I do, I just wished you were coming. We've spent so much time apart already."

"Oh sweetie, I know, but I already made the reservations and with the sweet deal, I can't change them, but I promise we'll take a trip, just you and I."

"You promise?" she whined.

"Of course."

Mackenzie didn't like the fact that she would have to spend the entire weekend with Ginger. It was obvious that she was a sneak and manipulative. *How dare she call Julian and apologize when it had been her idea to show up unannounced to the event?*

Chapter Twelve

Julian and Mackenzie arrived in Dallas a little after 3 pm in hopes that they would handle things and then get back home. Jonathan had promised them that things should run rather smoothly, and they were hoping that it would.

"He said we should check in and then meet him at his office no later than five."

"I'm glad he didn't mind meeting us on a Friday. Most attorneys don't even come in on Fridays."

"Tell me about it." Julian smiled because he knew all too well about that notion. Fridays were he and Ken's day to play golf or just review cases—nothing major.

"Did you bring her documents?"

"Yep, the ones that they sent from the courthouse has my name on it as her birth mother."

"Great. The hotel is not too far from his office on Stemmons. We should head over before it's too late."

Mackenzie and Julian checked into their hotel and freshened up before heading to see Jonathan.

"Hey Julian, Mrs. Taylor. Come on in; I've been expecting you."

"Hey, Jonathan, how's everything going? I'm glad you could help."

"Oh, that's no problem. You two have a seat and let me take a look at those documents."

Mackenzie handed the tall mulatto man the documents and took a seat beside Julian. She surveyed his elegantly decorated office and waited patiently for feedback.

The palms of her hands were sweaty, and she still had an occasional stomachache whenever she thought of her upcoming weekend with Ginger. She wanted more than anything to focus on Jay-Jay and getting her back, but all she could see was Ginger and her smoky eyes.

"So, Counselor, what do you think?"

"Well, the good news is that these are real documents, so we won't have to worry about that being a problem. My next concern is the father. Is there any reason that he would side with Erasmus and her family? Would he try and stop you from getting full custody of Jay-Jay?"

"I thought we had a problem," Mackenzie replied, with a sense of relief. "He doesn't even know that Jay-Jay exists. He made me promise that I would abort her; and, I promised that I would. I haven't seen or heard from him since."

"Okay, then we won't have a problem there. Next concern: is there any reason why her family could say that you are an unfit mother? I mean *any* reason, because I'll need to know just in case they try to dig something up."

Mackenzie felt a little awkward. She looked at Julian, who signaled to her to go ahead.

"Erasmus and I used to be lovers," she responded quietly. "We raised Jay-Jay together until she left and took Jay-Jay with her. There were drugs involved on both our parts. When they left, I sobered up, put myself through college and law school, and the last time she came by with Jay-Jay, she had sobered up as well."

"Are you sure? Because this could make or break the case."

"Sure about the story, or if she's sobered up?"

"Both."

"I'm sure about the story, and like I said, the last time she showed up she said she was sober. She looked and acted sober."

"Did you two hook back up for any reason, or was it platonic and for the sake of Jay-Jay?" Mackenzie was startled at his barrage of questions. She had to think fast and respond without letting on about her last sexual encounter with Erasmus.

"It was for the sake of Jay-Jay, and it was platonic. She needed help with taking care of her, so I helped her find a job and a place for the two of them to stay."

"And that's right before she was arrested, right?"

"Right, but she was cleared."

"Right." He nodded, then looked at Julian.

"Well, I'd say this is a winner. Just give me a week or so to get this turned in. We'll wait for a response, which will probably take 7–10 business days, and then we'll go from there.

"My guess is that they will relinquish their ties and turn Jay-Jay over to you. It seems as though Erasmus would want it that way, wouldn't you say, Mrs. Taylor?"

"I sure hope so," she replied, relieved that the session was over.

"I do as well. So, what are you guys going to get into this weekend?"

"We haven't planned anything—probably check out Nick and Tiphane and go see her family and then head back."

"Give me a call before you guys head back. Okay?"

"Sure, and thanks again. Just send the bill to Ken and I."

"Oh don't worry, this one's on the house."

"Thanks man, we really appreciate this."

"Yes, we do. Thank you so much," Mackenzie replied, as she extended her hand.

"Mrs. Taylor, it is my pleasure." He smiled and shook her hand.

They exited his office with the hope of getting Jay-Jay back and went to meet Nick and Tiphane for drinks.

The Caribbean Bar and Grill was still alive and kicking. Nick and Tiphane were welcoming their first child and enjoying married life. They sat and talked for hours before heading back to rest up for shopping and lunch with Aunt Cecile and the twins on Saturday.

Part III:

It Takes Two

Chapter Thirteen

"*H*oney, are you sure you and Ken won't join us in Miami?" *His wife is after me honey, she wants to get with me please don't send me out to the "dogs" or "bitch" or whatever the hell she is!*

"Oh sweetie, you'll be fine. Besides, Ken and I have just linked a lucrative case."

"Really? Do I even want to know any of the details?"

"Probably not, sweetie. I'm afraid this one may hit too close to home."

Mackenzie widened her eyes and adjusted her stance. "How so?" she asked.

"Well, this time we have a female client, and of course she's being blackmailed about her lifestyle by a former lover, who's threatening to go to the press."

"You've got to be kidding me?"

"Baby, I wish I were. I would have never thought that she would be, but she is full fledged."

"A lesbian, Julian?" *Damn! What the fuck is this some sort of a conspiracy?*

"Yep, but if you saw her you wouldn't think so. I mean, everything that she's acted in, she's been the girl who gets the guy and lives happily ever after. So, you can image the look on our faces. Ken and I were both floored, to say the least." *Yeah, Ken would be floored if he knew his wife just had her tongue down my throat!*

"I told you this would happen," she said. "I guess you guys will be busy then? Is she a black actress?" *Sure her name isn't Ginger Smallwood 'cause that bitch is acting like she's straight; hell, had me fooled and I should know!*

"Yeah, she is, and yeah, at least for two weeks. She just wants us to make a deal so this can go away quietly."

"Do you think that it will?"

"For the amount that we are charging her, it better." He laughed as Mackenzie remembered her date with Ginger.

"The driver should be here in about twenty minutes. You sure you have everything?"

"Everything except you." She smiled at Julian and he smiled back.

"Come kiss me goodbye, sweetie. You know I'll miss you."

They kissed and hugged until the driver arrived and Ginger showed up. Julian sent them off with lots of love and with no inclination of their level of comfort or discomfort for one another. They both placed their luggage in the trunk with the help of the driver and Julian and quietly sat in the car, ignoring each other and listening to the light Jazz in the background as the driver made small talk until they made it to the airport.

"Well hello, Ms. Mackenzie, and how have you been?"

"Just fine, Ms. Ginger, and you?"

"Just worried about you, that's all."

"I've been just fine. Julian and I have both been fine."

"I'm happy to hear it. So, are you ready for our trip?"

"I guess so. I could really use the pampering."

Ginger looked deep into Mackenzie eyes and smiled. "I look forward to it as well."

"Listen, Ginger, before we even board this plane, let's get something straight. I don't know what you heard, but I love my husband, and there is nothing that you can do for me. I'm not even interested in being your friend. I'm really being forced on this trip, if you must know."

"Okay wait now, let's start over. Mackenzie, I apologize for the other night. We both had way too much to drink, and I thought I saw something that obviously wasn't there. I need this vacation as well, trust me. So, we can just forget everything else and concentrate on getting pampered."

"Ginger, I'm serious. I don't want any of your shit because that shit you pulled was not cute, or cool."

"You have my word. Now, let's board this plane and have some wine or something."

"The last time you said that, things didn't go so well," Mackenzie said, as she paused with her carry-on in tow.

"You're right. We'll have some coffee or tea, huh?"

"Now that's much better," Mackenzie said, and they boarded the 747 to Miami International airport.

They sipped on coffee and tea and laughed at the horror stories that Ginger shared about the emergency room when she was an intern. And as much as Mackenzie hated it, she was beginning to like Ginger and the possibility of a friendship between the two of them.

When they arrived in the beautiful city of Miami Beach, they had a rental awaiting them. They drove down the turnpike to their resort and were in complete awe of its stature. The huge, twenty-story, condo-style resort overlooked the beach and was fully equipped with a spa, restaurant, olympic size pool, and top-notch room service.

They quickly put up their belongings and changed into their swimsuits, then hurried down to the beach. The full moon lit up the ocean and for a moment, Mackenzie wished that she could grab Julian by the hand and walk along the ocean side.

"Isn't this romantic, Mackenzie?"

"Yeah, isn't it? I wish Julian was here."

"Yeah, it would be nice, huh?"

"Come, let's get a bite to eat."

"Sure, I can use a bite."

They walked side by side and went over to Jimmy Johnson's eatery on the boardwalk. Then sat quietly and sipped on house wine until the waiter bought them their entrees.

"We should go dancing later. That would be nice."

"Yeah, but where would we go?"

"Well, I searched the net before we left, and I have a list of different clubs. I want to go Salsa dancing. What about you?"

"I've never Salsa danced, but I wouldn't mind trying it."

"Cool, let's finish dinner, then we'll change and head to the strip."

"The strip?"

"Yeah, it's a strip of clubs," Ginger said, with a hint of enthusiasm.

"Wow, I can't wait." Mackenzie was eager to dance again, reliving her days back in Dallas when she often let her hair down and danced the night away.

They enjoyed dinner with a few more laughs, then headed to their room to change. They dolled themselves up with a little makeup and took a cab to the strip, which was about a mile and a half away from their hotel.

The scene was a replica of Mardi Gras, with tourists filling the streets, happy off of wine and many other spirits.

They quickly located the Salsa club, which was packed with all types of people. They followed the people to the dance floor and quickly joined in, trying to Salsa dance. They giggled at their two left feet and watched others trying to learn. In between several trips to the bartender and a couple of guys who felt sorry for them and their lack of rhythm, they finally mastered the art of Salsa dancing and danced until the wee hours of the morning before catching a cab back to their room.

"God, I haven't had that much fun in along time, Mackenzie. Thanks, I really needed that."

"Oh girl, it was all you. *I* needed that."

"Mackenzie, you are so crazy—but you can dance, girl, moving those hips all over the place."

"Oh please, I was trying to keep up with you and what's his name. You two tore up the floor, all sweaty and all over each other."

Ginger laughed at Mackenzie's erotic rendition of her and her male friend at the club. While she undressed, Mackenzie laughed to herself.

"You'd better not tell Ken; he would die if he knew."

"*Blackmail*," Mackenzie said, as she laughed at Ginger.

"Mackenzie, come here; you have something on you."

"Oh no , you just want to get close to me, Ms. Ginger. Didn't I tell you that I read minds? I know what you want," Mackenzie said, teasing Ginger with her eyes. The many drinks that they'd both consumed were having an effect on Mackenzie.

"No, really, you have a string or something on the back of your heel."

"Ms. Ginger, no thank you. And can't you be more charming than that?"

Ginger walked over to Mackenzie and stepped on the toilet tissue that was attached to her heel, then smiled at Mackenzie.

"Oops! I didn't even see that. You mean I made it all the way home without noticing?" She looked down at her classy summer heal with rhinestones that glistened, as Ginger stood by and watched a fascinated Mackenzie looking at her shoes.

She looked up at Ginger as she began to walk off, her toned body a perfect silhouette in a strapless fancy bra with matching low-rise thong panties.

"Ginger, wait," she said, pulling her close. "I want to see something." She pulled her into her, catching Ginger off guard and looked back into her eyes, then pushed her away, still teasing her, allowing herself to go where she had promised she would never go again.

But to her surprise, Ginger pulled her back and pulled her mouth into hers, and they kissed, open mouthed, with passion, questions, wants, and needs.

"I can't do this to Julian," Mackenzie softly whispered, yet wanting to go further. She knew it was already too late. The crime had been committed—she was taken by Ginger. *Shit!*

"Ginger, did you hear me, I can't do this to Julian." *Although my body is saying something totally different!*

"I hear you, but your body is saying otherwise. Mackenzie, I've been paying attention. We both know what this is about," she said, this time looking deep into her eyes.

"No, I really can't. He doesn't deserve this. No one does," Mackenzie said, as she attempted to get away from the heat that had risen between the two of them.

Mackenzie removed herself from Ginger's powerful embrace and quickly came to her senses. She looked over at Ginger and saw the passion in her eyes something in her wanted Ginger; it was stirring fiercely inside, driving her crazy. She knew it too.

Ginger wasn't like anyone she had ever experienced before. She was powerful, in control, and she could seduce Mackenzie with her eyes alone. She allowed Mackenzie to feel weak and vulnerable. She needed to be seduced.

Chapter Fourteen

"So, now that it's morning, what shall we do?" Mackenzie asked, as she curled up next to Ginger.

"Have breakfast I guess."

"Ginger, that's not what I mean, and you know it."

"I need to find my stash; I have a terrible headache."

"Do you smoke every time you get a headache? Just curious?"

"What's with the questions, Mackenzie? You knew that I smoked, so what gives?"

"Whoa, wait a sec, I was just asking a question; you don't have to bite my head off."

"Well, it was dumb question."

"What? What's your problem? I thought you were okay with this?"

"With what?—your *rules of engagement?* Yeah, right."

"Ginger, we are both married women; what do you expect?"

"Doesn't matter, you couldn't handle it anyway."

"Is that a challenge Ginger? I mean this isn't some game."

"Did Julian call you last night or this morning?" Ginger asked.

"Where is that coming from?"

"Just answer the question."

"Well, you were here with me, did he?"

"Answer the question, Mackenzie."

"Don't tell me to answer the damn question! You were here with me, *you* answer it." Mackenzie rolled out of bed and retrieved her robe, then slammed the door as she walked into the bathroom.

She didn't quite understand Ginger's point and wasn't in the mood for any games. She had no idea what Ginger was up to, and that frightened her.

She turned the shower on full blast and dropped her robe and showered. She had realized that she had done it again. She had allowed herself to become involved with another woman. *Another fuckin' woman!*

"Why?" she said over and over to herself. "Why?"

There was a knock at the door as Mackenzie stepped out of the shower and began to dry off. Still recanting in her head the sexual escapade that had taken place most of the night and early morning.

"Can I come in?" Ginger asked, sounding remorseful.

"I'll be out in a sec."

The door opened slightly as Ginger walked in, fully dressed, with a glass of water. "No thanks," Mackenzie said, without looking at her and continuing to dry her body and lather up with scented cucumber lotion.

"He didn't call because he's cheating on you, Mackenzie."

"What? Ginger, do not start your manipulation. I don't want to hear it."

"I can't do this alone, Mackenzie."

"You seemed to be doing fine." She continued to lotion her legs and feet attempting to ignore Ginger's games.

"I'm asking Ken for a divorce when we get back."

"You're what? Why Ginger? This was only one night. You said you could handle it with no strings attached. Did you lie to me?" Mackenzie asked as the steam began to leave the bathroom with the lotion in her hands.

"I've got to lie down, this pain is killing me."

"That's it. You drop a bomb like that and now you want to retreat? And where are my things?" Mackenzie asked as she finished with her lotion and nervously tried to remember where she had put her clothes.

"Not right now, Mackenzie. And, you put your clothes in the top drawer before we finally went to bed. Remember?"

"OK, I get your point, but Ginger, you said you could handle this being a one-night stand, now you come to me with all of this stuff. What about our husbands?" Mackenzie walked past her and located her clothes. She quickly put on some jeans without any panties, a tank, and her flip-flops.

"I told you, you don't want to accept it."

"Ginger, why am I supposed to believe that he's cheating on me from you, when we just slept together? How realistic is that?"

Ginger stared down at Mackenzie with a pitiful look on her face and shook her head.

"Where is he, Mackenzie? Huh, where is he?"

"Shit, home where he said he would be. They're working on a case."

"Who's working on a case?"

"Julian and Ken—who else, Ginger?"

"Oh really? And which case might that be?"

"What is this, Ginger, twenty fuckin' questions? What's your problem? You can't handle being second? Damn! This is all that I can give you."

Ginger ignored Mackenzie's tone and words and walked over to the phone. She picked up the receiver and dialed straight through.

"Hello dear . . . just fine. Hang on a sec." She handed the phone to a surprised Mackenzie.

"Hello? Oh hey, Ken, how are you? Yeah, I'm enjoying myself . . . relaxing, taking in a little sun, catching up on rest." She looked at Ginger, who motioned for her to ask.

"So, you guys getting much work done on that case?" she asked, as she looked at Ginger.

"Oh, you guys are finished...You didn't have one to work on? I thought you two had another high profile case with a female celebrity... It ended a week ago? Oh, I guess I just misunderstood Julian.

"He's not here with me. I'm here with Ginger, remember? It was you guys' idea to send us here . . . You didn't?"

"Julian said that you two were taking a weekend trip to the coast or something. I was wondering what Ginger was doing there to be honest." Ken said over the phone.

"Ken, I thought you and Julian set this up for us. So you're saying you had no idea about this trip?"

"Well, as you can see, Ginger likes to spend a great deal of time alone. I just figured she was taking a break from her job—that's what she told me."

"Hang on I'll put her back on." Mackenzie handed her the phone and then sat on the bed and waited for her to end their conversation.

"We'll talk when I return, Ken. That's fine. Good-bye," Ginger said, as she hung up the phone.

"So wait, how did you know about this trip?" Mackenzie asked before she could hang up the phone.

"Julian called and asked if I would accompany you for a weekend retreat—his treat. I agreed."

"How do you know he's cheating, Ginger? And don't give me any bullshit either."

"What are you, blind? You saw the way his secretary was all over him. It was obvious, Mackenzie—don't be stupid."

"Don't throw that word around here like you have the right to use it. I trust my husband okay."

"Fine, Mackenzie, stay in denial. I'm leaving Ken because I can't live a lie anymore. You do what you have to do."

"Whatever, Ginger, we don't need to discuss this anymore. Let's just forget what happened here and call it a day."

"Fine with me, but don't say I didn't tell you when this blows up in your face."

"Tell me what? You've made accusations; you have no proof. Hell, I slept with you last night. Why should I believe you? Let's be serious."

"Precisely. You slept with me last night. You whispered my name; you held on to me; and where was your damn husband? With some damn Spanish immigrant, fucking her brains out. You said that you loved the—"

Mackenzie pulled back her slender arm and slapped Ginger as hard as she could. Tears flowed from her eyes, and she wanted to die rather than to hear those words.

Ginger held her face with her mouth wide open, picked up her purse and gathered her room key, and abruptly left.

"Ginger, wait," Mackenzie called out, as her silhouette rushed through the door.

Mackenzie hurried, grabbed her purse and room-card, and exited after Ginger. The door slammed at her back as she began to jog down the hall, but her jog was interrupted as Ginger lie helplessly on the floor, clutching her head.

"Ginger, are you okay?" she said, as she ran to her. Ginger squirmed and murmured as Mackenzie's heart began to race.

"Ginger, say something," she yelled, as a young couple looked on. "Something is wrong with my friend, can you help me, please!"

The freshly tanned couple turned their faces and sped up their pace.

Oh my God, she's gonna die, Mackenzie thought to herself, as she looked around frantically.

"I'm okay," Ginger whispered. "I'm okay."

"No, I need to call somebody."

"Mackenzie listen, I'm okay. I just need to lie down," she said, as she opened her eyes.

"Are you sure?" Mackenzie asked, uncertain as to what to do next. But Ginger reached out for her hand as Mackenzie took it and struggled to help her up.

"I just need to lie down," Ginger said again softly, as Mackenzie opened the door and led her to the bed.

"Should I go and get some tea or call for room service?"

Ginger nodded her head as she slipped into bed and curled up while her head sank deep into the pillows. Mackenzie slipped off her shoes and walked to the phone. She ordered some fresh fruit and hot, green tea.

She sat on the chaise lounge, watching Ginger as she drifted off to sleep and waited for room service. *I can't believe I did that. God, I hope this isn't my fault.*

Mackenzie sat and wondered what she should do to help Ginger. *Maybe I should call Ken, or maybe Julian...what if she doesn't wake up?* Her mind was rattled, and she jumped when there was a knock at the door.

She rushed to the door and asked, "Who is it?"

"Room service."

She unlatched the door and greeted the bellboy, quickly taking the tray and rushing to check on Ginger. She paid no attention to the bellboy that stood there after she retrieved the tray, expecting a tip for his deed.

"Ginger, wake up. The tea is here," she said, as she sat beside a curled up Ginger who breathed in an out, at rest.

"Ginger, sweetie, wake up," she said, as she lightly nudged her.

Ginger moved some as Mackenzie patiently waited for her to sit up. She poked her head up, trying to gather her whereabouts. "The tea is here," Mackenzie said again, as Ginger put her head back down.

"I'm tired," she said, as she looked at the wall.

"Why don't you have a little tea? It will make you rest better."

"I need my bag."

Mackenzie looked across the room and saw Ginger's hobo Louis vuitton. She handed it to her as Ginger sat up and began to search its contents. She dumped it upside down and grabbed a zip-lock baggy full of marijuana.

"Are you sure you need that?"

Ginger smiled at Mackenzie and continued to light up her joint. She sucked on it for a couple of minutes with long, slow drags, inhaling deeply as she blew the smoke out of her nose. Mackenzie watched as she continued her routine, which lasted for five or so minutes.

When she finished, she left the contents of her purse on the bed, put out her joint, and said, "Wake me up in a couple of hours."

She's a weed head, Mackenzie thought to herself, as she went back to lie on the chaise. She turned on the TV and flipped through the various channels before falling asleep herself.

Chapter Fifteen

"What time is it?" Mackenzie asked, as Ginger stared down at her.

"A little after seven maybe, 7:15 or so."

"How are you feeling?" Mackenzie asked, sitting up as Ginger sat down beside her.

"Much better," she said, looking down at the floor.

"So, what was wrong?"

"Just a migraine," she replied. She looked at Mackenzie with her golden girl smile.

"Are you sure? It seemed pretty serious. Maybe we should call Ken."

"Mackenzie, I'm fine. Thanks for being here for me."

"Ginger, I'm sorry about this morning."

"You don't have to apologize, I overstepped my boundaries. I shouldn't have."

"I know, but I share part of the blame, too. We shouldn't have let last night happen."

"Agreed, so can we just forget it and be friends?" Ginger asked, flashing her golden girl smile once again.

"Sure. So, did you try any of that tea that the bellboy brought up?"

"Yeah, I tried a little bit," Ginger said, as she shifted her eyes back to the floor.

"Liar," Mackenzie said with a chuckle.

"I know, right, but you're up now, you can have some with me."

"Nice save," Mackenzie said, as she got up and called room service for more hot tea.

"Well, it's not like it's cold outside."

"I know that, but it soothes the insides, silly. You've never tried green tea?"

"Nope. But if you insist that it's so good, I guess I'll try some."

"I'm telling you, girl, it's wonderful and far better than that stinkin' crap you smoke."

"Hey, hey, don't hate, participate," Ginger said with a smile.

"Dr. Smallwood, need I remind you of your profession?" Mackenzie said with a smirk. "And trust me, I know all about the drug scene."

Ginger opened her mouth in awe. "Give it up," she said, as she plopped back down on the chaise, wanting to hear the details.

"Calm down, calm down—that life is far gone."

"So, I want to hear about it. Come on, girl, give it up."

"Okay, it's not like you can blackmail me—you smoke, too."

"You smoke?"

"No, silly, but I've tried it before."

"Really?"

"Yep," Mackenzie said, as she stretched out on the floor.

"I never thought I would smoke the stuff, I always looked down on people that did."

"So, why do you?"

"Long story, and besides, it's your night to dish."

Mackenzie smiled. "You're so nosy, Ginger."

"I know, now give it."

"It was a very long time ago. My good friend and I, Erasmus, were acid heads—well, at least I was, yeah, and I guess I took ecstasy, too."

"You? You're kidding? I can't believe it."

"Yeah, I was a bit much at one time."

"But you're an attorney. Ken said at one time you were very successful at your job."

"Was, I still am, I'm just taking a little break, Ms. *Girl*."

"So, you and your friend got high together?"

"Something like that."

"Wow, I had no idea, but I see why you have no desire for my stuff. It would probably bore you."

"Ha, ha very funny but it's called deliverance, ever heard of it?"

"Is that what they're calling re-hab now?"

"Oh, Ms. Ginger, you are on a roll. You've got jokes, huh?"

"Nah, just kidding. I understand, we all have a past or two."

"So, what's your story?"

"For me, the drugs . . . I don't know. But everything else, well, I guess I fell in love with my best friend and to be honest, my life has never been the same. That's the short version." She laughed.

"I take it you're not speaking of Ken?"

"I wish I were. Ken's cool, but I just can't do the married thing anymore. I need my freedom."

"I had no idea. I thought you two were happy."

"Well he is, but it takes two to make a relationship work—or better yet to make a marriage work."

"So, who's this best friend? Do you still see her?"

Ginger shook her head no. "I've never been the same since then though."

"I guess I didn't make things any better."

"Nope, I'm sorry, Mackenzie, the first time we hung out was so familiar. I was so comfortable with you and relaxed. The kiss just seemed like the next thing to do. It reminded me of when Shae and I met and became friends our freshmen year in college."

"Really? But I was just trying to be a friend. I guess Julian had me so upset. I didn't realize I was sending mixed messages."

"I know. I just became too comfortable, and this whole marriage thing . . . I feel so caged."

"So, what happened with you and Shae?"

"Ms. Priss the basketball star?"

"Is that Shae?"

"Yeah, that was her nickname, Ms. Priss. She was from Alabama—

beautiful, tall, model type, just had the *Jones* for basketball. She played forward or post or something like that at our college.

"I still don't know how we wound up being roommates. Oh that's right, she didn't want to be around the other basketball girls, said they were too manly, and if the coach didn't fix her sleeping quarters she was quitting.

"I was supposed to be in a dorm by myself 'cause I was such a loner. But the dorm manager asked if I wouldn't mind since she would be gone a lot with basketball, so I agreed.

"Her accent was sharp and distinct. I remember just staring at her whenever she spoke, and she was such a lady, getting her toes done before games, hair always relaxed—she stood out for sure."

"I bet she did. So, how did you two become lovers?"

"Aren't we being nosy?"

"That's right, now you give it."

Ginger laughed.

"She didn't go home that summer and neither did I. I wanted to get ahead; she wanted to work out with the football team. We started working out every other night, trying to tighten up our abs.

"We talked about the guys on campus—mostly the football guys—who was sexy, who wasn't, who we would date, and who we definitely wouldn't date. Before the summer ended, we were talking about what turned us on sexually, staying up later and later every night having *girl talk*.

"When school started again, we were closer. When I did my laundry I did hers; when she was given extra perks for playing ball, she always made sure she got enough for me, not that I needed it, but it was like our friendship ties.

"She invited me to their first home game and made sure I was sitting pretty much front court. I'll never forget seeing her play—she was totally different; she was a monster on that court. Someone that beautiful and dainty made me want to check underneath her shorts to see if she was a woman when she was out there. I think I fell in love with her that night."

"You think? I was kinda of thinking the *girl talk* got you," Mackenzie said with a smile.

"No, I'm pretty sure it was that night we stayed up all night talking about the game. I had met this guy, Ken, that summer, and we had been kind of dating whenever either of us had had the time. We were supposed to go out after the game but I just couldn't leave Shae; I wanted to talk and just hang out.

"We cut the ringer off and sat on her bed. She peeled off her basketball stuff, too tired to put anything else on, and just laid there. We talked until the sun came up about basketball, her hoop dreams, and my medical dreams. I told her about growing up an only child and being so lonely.

"By the time the sun came up, we curled up next to each other and fell asleep. I was so comfortable with her she was like my protection. We talked about so much. We understood each other in a way that was surreal. Well it was Sunday, so we had no class. We woke up around three and lounged around in our t-shirts and panties.

"We ordered pizza, washed each other's hair, and she painted my nails while we listened to an Annie Lennox CD, which was on repeat, then laid on the floor with our heads opposite one another. She put her foot on my stomach and just rested it there. I massaged it, playing with her toes in between Annie Lennox singing "Why." It was quiet except for the music. We both had let out so much already, I guess we were trying to take it all in. I just wanted her to hold me but didn't know how to express that I remember wanting to just hide in her arms while she held me."

"I actually thought that she had fallen asleep, so I stopped and just stared up at the ceiling fighting the pain our talk had caused. She rubbed her foot against my stomach, and I was literally turned on. It scared the shit out of me. I was burning with sexual tension and confused I didn't know where to place my feelings."

"'I thought you were sleeping,' I said to her. 'No, are you tired?' she asked.

"'No, you want me to keep rubbing?' I asked before I even realized what I was saying.'"This time, she rubbed her foot even harder against my stomach, and I know I was wet.

"*We are playing with fire*, I thought to myself…*playing with fire*.

"She rubbed her foot against my stomach and then teased my breast, lightly touching them, then really touching them with her strong toes. Oh god was I wet. I didn't know what to do I was so confused, but it felt *soooo* good. It felt safe. I grabbed her foot and stopped her, then massaged her foot with intensity, she sat up and pushed her foot into me like she wanted me to take it and do whatever I wanted to do with it.

"And I did, I put it between my legs and used it to fulfill my pleasures while she watched, smiling until I climaxed. I ain't been no good since, girl, I'm telling you."

"Wow, that's powerful."

"Tell me about it. That orgasm made the beast in me come out. I wanted to be on top of her and touch every part of her body. Her body was so beautiful and toned, muscular yet soft. She had the smoothest skin, the color of cocoa butter, and thick, wavy hair. When she let it down, she looked like a mermaid.

"We found each other's vaginas and rubbed them together. She grabbed my ass, pulling me further and further as our juices mixed, and it was like my vagina squirted out hot liquids and hers did the same because it was like hell down there when we both let out moans as we came. I have never been the same woman since. I am serious. It was powerful."

"So, how does Ken fit into all of this?"

"Well, we had to carry on like things were normal between us. She was worried about her teammates; I was worried about my image. My parents would die if they found that out. So we hid, sleeping in the same bed night after night. We were best friends dating but no one ever suspected it. I was at all of her home games and sat front row.

"Ken and I became close, but I never told him about her. He was a cover up until our junior year came. Well, I guess it was the summer before we were to become seniors. She went to play for some special league that she was selected for. Ken and I became closer; I guess he was a lot older, already doing his law thing, getting established, and I was becoming more focused on my future goals trying to get into med school early.

"When she came back, I was spending more time with Ken trying to get into Columbia. We still had girl talk and slept together, but the intensity was gone. I had fallen for Ken. Well, I guess the power that he exuded when he was on campus."

"Did you tell her?"

"No, but she knew. She moved out one weekend without telling me. I went to the gym to find out what was up, but she wouldn't talk. I didn't want to make a scene either, so we just looked at each other with this huge amount of hurt, and I said bye and left."

"Did you still see her on campus?"

"Yeah, but it was like seeing a total stranger. She didn't even acknowledge my existence. Graduation day, we sat right behind each other, and she completely ignored me. I had met her parents once before so I spoke to them while she conveniently walked off and that was it. They never asked, and I didn't bother to tell."

"So, what happened to her? I mean, have you two reconciled at all or at least made peace?"

"Nope. She plays for the WNBA now."

Mackenzie squinted her eyes, trying to figure out who Shae was. "I bet her name wasn't Shae, was it?" she asked.

"Right again, kiddo."

"You dog."

"Well, I have to protect the innocent."

"Yeah, I guess you're right. So, have you seen her lately? Is that why you want a divorce from Ken?"

"No, I've been lying to myself. That was the best companionship I've ever had. Ken was good for getting me through med school and getting where we both are now, but it's been almost a year of a marriage that has been hell, let alone all of the years we've been together."

"Does he know about *Shae?*"

"No, but he knows that I'm at my wits end."

"So, what about the headaches? You think it's anxiety maybe missing her."

"No, I wish sweetie—it's more complicated than that."

"The headaches or Shae?"

"Nosy Rosy."

"What are you going to do?" Mackenzie asked, as she stared up at Ginger resting on the chaise.

"About what?" she replied, twirling her thumbs.

"About Shae? Stay on the same page, Mary."

"Who the hell is Mary?" Ginger asked.

"Oh god, never mind."

"I need a smoke. Do you mind grabbing my stash?"

"Ginger, you have gotta find a better hobby. I mean really, this is a bit much."

"Mackenzie, don't start, dear friend. I was just beginning to like you."

"I don't recall you telling me how you started this habit. Did you guys get high together?"

"No, we weren't like you and your buddy. It was all love."

"Well, we were in love, too, just got caught up."

"Really?" Ginger said, as she sat up and looked at Mackenzie.

"I mean we were good friends."

"You lie, you lie, you lie."

"I can't believe I just said that."

"I can't believe you weren't going to tell me. I knew it was something. You just kissed like an ole' pro."

"Thanks a lot, Ginger, but as you can see, I'm not having a relapse. That life is over for me."

"Un huh."

"Ginger, I'm serious. I want my marriage to work. I almost lost him once. I don't want to go through that again."

"What happened?"

"Not telling him about my past and it blew up in my face."

"I see. Well, I'm just getting a divorce, then I'll figure out my next move."

"Yeah right. You know you're probably gonna go looking for Shae."

"Cute Mackenzie, real cute. Now, are you going to get my bag?"

"Lazy girl," Mackenzie said, as she got up and strolled over to the bed to get Ginger's stash.

"Agreed. So, are we heading out for something to eat tonight?"

"I don't know, are you up for it?"

"It's late, but I still want to. But I have to get a little smoke first."

"Ms. Ginger, you are too much," Mackenzie said, as she tossed the stash of marijuana to Ginger.

"Thank you, sweetie."

"So, what about your family? Do they know about you?"

"Girl, no. My father is a physician in our hometown. Mom is the president of the usher board at our church and happy homemaker. They would die if I told them."

"You haven't told anyone? You don't have anyone you could process this stuff with? I'm sure your parents would understand; they're your folks."

"Mackenzie, growing up in my household was cold. I hated my father and despised my Momma for being so damn dumb! My father was awful. God, I cringe in his presence to this day."

"Damn, that's deep. I see why you broke loose in college. Is he why you went into medicine?"

"I wouldn't call it breaking loose. I was learning to love myself and be loved. Shae was a true friend. She knows my deepest secrets and not once has she treated me any different. Even when we stopped speaking, if I needed her, I mean truly needed her, she would have been there for me.

"My parents, they were both clueless. I guess too caught up in their own sins. I went into medicine to show that bastard that I could do something with my life. He was so hard on me."

"Really? What sins?"

"Infidelity and ignorance!"

"That's tough. My dad just left us. I guess it was best that he did instead of having to watch him dog my mom out."

"Do you speak to them much?"

"Nah, they're both deceased."

"Sorry, I wish mine were both dead."

"Ginger, don't say that. At no age is losing a parent easy. It's tough—believe me, really tough."

There was silence for a moment.

"So, which one did you look like?" Mackenzie asked.

"I've been told that they are both very beautiful people, I guess. Many have said I'm tall like my father and pretty like my mother."

"I looked like my mother, too."

"Yeah, well I'm gonna shower," Ginger said, getting up and taking her baggy to the bathroom with her.

"Okay, I'll be in after you."

Chapter Sixteen

"Come on, Mackenzie, it will be fun."

"Ginger, it's dark down there. We can walk on the beach in the morning."

"I won't let anything get you, come on, kiddo," Ginger pleaded, then led Mackenzie down the sandy stairs to the shoreline.

"The weather's nice."

"It is, just a little dark."

"The full moon is gone—just the tiny stars trying to give off as much light as they can. Like tiny angels doing the best that they can."

"Thinking about your patients?"

"Yeah, I miss those little angels. You want to do something crazy?" Ginger asked, as Mackenzie watched her bare feet make prints in the sand.

"It depends, 'Zena,'" Mackenzie said, folding her arms across her chest. Her white linen halter dress flowed in the night wind.

"Promise you won't say no?"

"Ginger, now I know you're crazy. Girl, I'll say yes and the next thing I know, we'll be in a heap of trouble," Mackenzie said with a giggle.

"It's legal—well, I think . . . you know, I'm not sure now that you mention it."

"See that, Ginger, I gotta watch you."

They shared a laugh.

"Let's go skinny dipping, Mackenzie. It'll be fun. I promise, just a little fun—memories you know."

"Skinny dipping, Ginger? That *is* illegal and what, do you work for this resort? Sounding like you're putting together a jingle."

"Oh, come on; we only live once. What do you say?"

Mackenzie sighed, looking at the pitiful face Ginger was purposely displaying. "Okay, but I'm not taking off my panties."

"You will," Ginger said happily, as Mackenzie began slipping out of her dress. "You know, it's not skinny dipping unless you take off everything," Ginger said with a wink. She took off her dress; she was naked underneath. Her tall, full, model's body casually strolled to the water as she jumped in, frolicking in the waves.

"Are you coming?" she called out, as Mackenzie tossed her panties on her dress and joined her for a night swim.

"It's warm," Mackenzie said, wiping the salt water from her face.

"Yeah, it's damn near erotic."

"Really now." Mackenzie giggled as Ginger grabbed her hand.

"Come on." Ginger pulled her underneath the clear water, still holding her hand as they swam in the dark sea. They came up for air when Mackenzie noticed that they swam horizontally and not further into the sea.

"This is so relaxing," Ginger said, as they both began to float.

"Yeah, this is. You ever done this with Shae?"

"No, we were in school and hiding of course. Never had time I guess, with basketball and my studies."

Mackenzie was silent, listening to the sounds of the ocean. "My body feels so good in here—weightless I suppose."

Ginger giggled. "Yeah, this is something—being wet, in more ways than one."

"You're so crazy, Ginger. I may have to sign you up for one of those sex rehab places."

"Oh, which one? The one you went to after your little friend broke your heart."

"She did not break my heart, thank you very much," Mackenzie said, laughing.

"Okay, whatever," Ginger said, looking away, her hair floating on top of the water.

She stood up, with the water dripping down her perfect breasts, pulling her hair up to show her beautiful facial features. Mackenzie eyes glazed over her perfect body, admiring her tight abs and perfect waist.

"Your body is flawless, girl. How do you do it?"

Ginger smiled and giggled at Mackenzie's excitement.

"You're not so bad yourself." She winked in the moonlight as Mackenzie stood and followed her out of the water. Her eyes trailed her body; she was lost in her thoughts.

"You okay?" Ginger asked, as she walked ahead of her, then sat at the edge of the shore.

"I'm fine, just enjoying the moment."

"I love letting the water wash away the sand in between my toes. It's like a cleansing is taking place." Ginger softly said.

"But if you just sit there, it comes back," Mackenzie said, as she traced the calf on Ginger's muscular leg.

"I know, you just have to know when to get up, wet, all the sand is washed away."

"Yeah, but then you'll be walking in the sand."

"But not sticky, muddy sand, just the sand that's inevitable, I suppose."

"There's always gonna be some sand—I guess the non-sticky, non-cruddy kind is the best."

Ginger leaned over and kissed Mackenzie on the side of her cheek. Mackenzie turned to face her, meeting her lips as they kissed softly.

"Maybe we should go back to the room," Mackenzie whispered, and Ginger looked deep into her eyes.

"This is fine. It will make a perfect memory, don't you think?" she said softly.

Mackenzie looked around the deserted beach. It was empty except for them, the slice of moon, and the stars and their angels, who were watching over them that night.

"Are you sure?" she asked Ginger, who was tracing her bottom lip.

"Your lips are so beautiful." She kissed them, savoring the taste. They kissed each other with wandering hands touching each other as passion crept in.

Ginger lay down in the water with her face in between Mackenzie legs; she opened them gently and washed the sand from her hands.

She pulled Mackenzie close and tasted her once again. The sounds of the ocean, the smell of the sea, with Ginger's moans in the background heated up Mackenzie all the more.

Ginger was a pro at this. Gliding her tongue against Mackenzie's grooves, she licked and sucked, going deep as the waves splashed against her perfect behind. Mackenzie hummed in ecstasy and watched Ginger as she moved her head to some sort of rhythm.

With her strong arms, she lifted Mackenzie up, cupping her into her strong hands.

"Shit," Mackenzie said, with cool air filling up her mouth. "Damn, you're good. Shit, that's the best I've ever had."

Ginger placed her head in her hands and smiled at Mackenzie's compliment. She began to peek further into Mackenzie special spot, playing with her, sticking her fingers inside, back and forth, and tracing her lips, which hung from beneath her closely shaven hairs.

"This is the most beautiful thing I've ever seen." she said, licking her index finger, and then twirling it around again. She teased her playing in its juices until Mackenzie tried to close her legs from the excitement. Ginger knew that she was recharged, as new juices began to mount up; pushing two fingers inside, which caused Mackenzie to jump. Ginger pressed against her G-spot, the one and same that her husband Julian had found already.

Ginger moved back in close, moving her tongue up and down across her while her two fingers provided the needed pressure. Her tongue danced in circles, and Mackenzie buried her long fingers in the sand, and she lost her breath, dizzy as she was about to explode.

Ginger worked harder at the joy she was giving Mackenzie, tasting her as though she was insatiable.

Mackenzie grabbed Ginger's head and pulled her in, until she came again. Sweat dripped from her moist body and she shook, biting down on her bottom lip.

"We better get going. Shit, the sun might catch us if you keep this up." Mackenzie said lowly as she tried to catch her breath.

Ginger laughed, rinsed the sand from between her breasts and legs, and got up. She walked over to their pile of clothes and Mackenzie followed slowly.

They dressed quietly while Mackenzie ignored the evidence that slid down her leg. *If she had a dick, I would be in trouble*, she thought to herself, as they headed back to the sandy steps leading off of the beach.

"Nice night," Ginger said.

"Yeah, it's a beautiful night," Mackenzie said, walking close beside Ginger.

"Nice show," a short, perverted, pot-bellied man said while clapping his hands as they walked along the boardwalk.

"I should have known we weren't alone," Mackenzie said, as Ginger reached for her hand.

"Memories, kiddo, memories," she said, and they walked back to their hotel.

Chapter Seventeen

"Come on, Ginger, this is our last night here. Let's go dancing. It'll be fun, plus, we can add it to our memories. Come on."

"I'm exhausted, Mackenzie. We can go when we make it home. I know a few spots."

Mackenzie's eyes widened. "Are you nuts? I can't go when we get home. Just my luck, I'll get busted."

"We'll just be going dancing, calm down, kiddo."

"I know, but come on, this place is different. It's our vacation. We have to make as many memories as possible. This weekend will *go down* in history." She winked at Ginger, who smiled at Mackenzie emphasis on "going down."

"Okay, you win. I saw a couple of places that are supposed to be top notch—even on a Sunday."

"Cool, let me get my wardrobe together. What's the dress code?"

"Chic, New York, LA flavor. That's what the website said. It's thirty to get in. Can you handle it?"

"Cute, Ginger. Real cute."

"It's ladies' night on Sundays. Sure you wanna try it out?"

"Yeah, come on. Let's get ready."

Two hours later, after much primping, shaving, waxing, and modeling, they both settled on a Versace, black, fitted dress for Ginger and a Dolce and Gabbana black dress for Mackenzie. Like two of Miami's elite class, they sashayed through the hotel lobby with all the right accessories and just enough perfume, as onlookers admired their beauty.

They caught the first available cab, taking them down to the South Beach limelight. "This is fine right here," Ginger said, and the two ladies stepped out into the warm, sensuous air.

"Here it is," Ginger said, as they stood in front of the busiest club with a line wrapped around the block. The patrons in line were all decked out in the finest attire and the latest fashions. It was casting call for all of the beautiful people in the world to come out tonight. There wasn't an ugly person in sight—not even the six-foot barrel of a security guard with a missing front tooth dressed in all black and stuffed in his clothes.

"What can I do for two of the most beautiful women here?"

Ginger smiled. *Luring him in*, Mackenzie thought.

"Are we now? But you haven't checked out all the other pretty women standing in line."

"You're right." He smiled, then leaned over and looked at all of the pretty girls standing there with attitudes.

"Y'all good," he said and let Mackenzie and Ginger in.

"Welcome to Club Z, and welcome to ladies' night," the vibrant female hostess said. She was barely dressed and had a weave that looked better than Janet Jackson's.

"We have coat check, purse check, and several rooms for private parties. Step to the cashier, and she'll take care of you."

"Not bad," Ginger said, nudging Mackenzie, who was taken in by the high-class décor and inhaling the club scent of marijuana and expensive cologne and perfumes.

They paid their thirty dollars and headed to the main area.

"This is hot," Mackenzie said, as the loud sounds of house music began to pump through their bodies.

"Yeah, this is," Ginger said over the loud music. She grabbed Mackenzie's hand and led her to the packed bar. They weaseled their way to the front, giving smiles and gently brushing up against several of the well-dressed men and women.

"What are you having?" the blond-headed bartender asked, looking like the rapper Eve.

"Four Mango Martini's," Ginger said, leaning her breasts forward. The bartender smiled and turned to make the drinks while she danced to the loud music that pumped even louder, mixing in hip hop over a hot house classic.

The Eve look-alike turned around with a smile and said, with a wink, "It's on the house." Mackenzie watched as the bartender grazed Ginger's hands as she took two drinks and passed them to Mackenzie, then grabbed hers, mouthing, "Thank you" to her fan.

They stood in the packed club, both hoping no one would spill their drinks, but that wasn't going to happen. These were professional party-goers who did everything to a rhythm.

They sipped their first Martini, then gulped the second before heading to the packed dance floor, groovin' to the latest Jay-Z cut. They got downright erotic to a spiced up remix of R. Kelly's "Feelin On My Booty," followed by "Fiesta."

They danced close with their sweat mixing sensuously, giggling while their audience watched and others gave their own shows.

At 5 am, they left the club, letting the cool breeze dry them off.

"So, what's up for the holidays?" Ginger asked, as they held hands and walked back to their hotel.

"I don't know; I guess I was going to cook. It will be our first married Thanksgiving and Christmas together. You're welcome to come."

"Nah, something like that is meant for couples."

"Ginger, it's the holidays—it's for friends and lovers." Ginger smiled. "Friends and lovers, huh?"

"Yeah," Mackenzie said, looking around at the nightlife that was still going on.

"Maybe I'll stop by, you never know," Ginger said, still holding Mackenzie's sweaty hands, rubbing her thumb across her palm.

"You'll be there. I just have a funny feeling you'll be there," Mackenzie said, squeezing Ginger's strong hand back.

They made it to their hotel as the sun snuck up on them. Then they showered together, rinsing each other's suds off and washing each other's hair before napping and rushing to the airport to catch their 1:15 flight back to San Francisco.

"What?" Ginger asked, as Mackenzie sat and stared at her on the huge 747 airplane, trying not to think about the last time she'd come home from a vacation to find out that her best friend was gone.

"Nothing, I was just wondering what's behind those simmering eyes."

"Simmering eyes, Mackenzie? What are you, a poet now?"

"Ha, ha. No, just wondering what you're thinking when you get that look."

"What look?"

"You know, when your eyelids come down and your eyes sort of whisper."

"Girl, you are so funny. It's probably the effects of the marijuana, crazy girl."

"Oh yeah, well now that the vacation is over, you'll have to give it a rest, huh?"

"Yeah, I guess I could."

"Yeah, you could," Mackenzie firmly stated, as they sat side by side on the airplane drinking orange juice and unwinding.

"So, why didn't you go into modeling? You're just so beautiful," Mackenzie asked Ginger.

"Thanks, but you are also. How come you didn't model?"

"Because I didn't know I was a bad bitch until my early twenties. Seems like you've always known. I know you notice how people look at you when you walk in a room."

"Well, thanks for the compliment, but I hardly ever paid any attention to my 'beauty.' It was actually my downfall, if you ask me."

"You're kidding, right?"

"Nope, but that's a long story."

"Ginger, it's a four-hour trip. We have time."

"Not today, but someday I'll tell you. I promise." Ginger said, tapping Mackenzie softly on her nose.

"Are you sure you want to do this, Ginger? I mean, maybe you guys can go to counseling," she asked, concerned about Ginger adamantly stating that she was asking Ken for a divorce.

"Mackenzie, I know you don't want to hear this, but it's a done deal. Maybe you should focus on you and Julian and your situation with his secretary."

"Ouch. That was a low blow."

"I mean really, Mackenzie, we haven't discussed what you are going to do."

"I'm going to stay with my husband and work things out. That's what I'm going to do."

"Well, if you need a place to stay, you know where to find me."

"Thanks, Ginger, but I'll be fine." *No she didn't.*

"Ginger how long have you and Ken been married just curious?"

"We've been together longer than we were married if that's what you want to know."

"I kinda figured that. But what I don't get is the fact that after all of that time you're just gonna throw it all away."

"Mackenzie we have been together for a long time. Have you ever been in a situation or relationship where you just weren't happy and it's just exhausting to keep up the charade? Well that's where I am, I'm exhausted."

Mackenzie turned away from Ginger and looked out of the tiny airplane window. The abundance of clouds moved swiftly as she pressed her head hard against the plexi-glass and dozed off to sleep while Ginger began to read. She knew all to well about being exhausted from a relationship that wasn't going anywhere.

Hours later, they arrived at the busy San Francisco airport, picked up their luggage, and went to meet their unsuspecting spouses in the arrival area.

"There's Ken," Mackenzie said, as they sashayed with their matching Louis Vuitton luggage.

"I wonder where Julian is?" she asked Ginger as they casually walked toward Ken.

"Ginger, where do you think Julian is?" Mackenzie asked, as Ken approached them.

"You don't want to know what I think. Hey Ken, how are you?" Ginger said, trying to sound nonchalant.

"Better now that my wife is home."

Ginger faked a half smile and handed Ken her things.

"Hey Ken, where's Julian?" Mackenzie asked, trying not to show any concern.

"Oh, he's at the office. He asked me to pick you up, said he'd be home in a couple of hours."

"Okay, you guys must be really busy."

"Well, I think he has some personal stuff he's taking care of, but rest assured, the money is in the bank."

"Well, I really don't care about the money, Ken; I just want my husband home so we can spend some time together."

"Oh, tell me about it. I've been dying to have the wife home." Ginger pulled back as Ken held her close and the three headed to his car.

"You ladies hungry?"

"Not really. I'm beat, and besides, the sunburn is killing my back," Mackenzie said.

"How about you, Ginger, feel like something to eat?"

"No, not really. I just want to get home."

"Well, I guess you two had plenty of fun down in Miami."

"Ken, let it rest."

"I thought we were going to take that trip, honey?"

"Ken, please, don't start."

The three of them continued to walk as Ginger and Ken talked back and forth.

"I thought we were taking the trip, Ginger. I get up and you're gone. But Julian knows where you are?"

"Ken, let it rest."

"And now you're too tired for dinner. How much of this do you expect me to take?"

Ginger stopped and pushed Ken's arm from around her waist. She yanked her things from his hand and said "Ken, I want a divorce. You don't have to take anything anymore." She walked off with her luggage and left Mackenzie and Ken both standing there in shock.

Chapter Eighteen

Ken stared at Ginger as she disappeared. "Come on," he said to Mackenzie. She followed him to his car with her luggage. They drove off in silence, dipping in and out of traffic.

"Where are we going?" she asked curtly.

"I still have to eat," he said, as they arrived at the Mexican restaurant *La La Linda*.

"Are you coming?"

"No, I'll wait here. Just hurry—I'm tired."

Ken shut the car door and zipped into the packed restaurant. Mackenzie sat and watched several other patrons come and go. She was starting to re-think Ken's offer for dinner when she saw Julian walking hand in hand with Anayelica.

Her stomach fell to her feet. She blinked several times to see if her eyes were deceiving her, but they weren't. He was leading her into the restaurant quickly so that no one would see them, and in stark contrast, she was smiling ear to ear in hopes that someone would—namely Mackenzie.

She ducked down into the car and fought back her tears. *Ginger was right*, was all that she could think. She sat there contemplating her next move. Part of her wanted to bolt out of the car and wring his neck while part of her wanted to crawl under a rock and hide.

She slid her cell phone out of her purse and quickly dialed Ginger's number. She had planned on erasing it but had forgotten. Now she was glad that she hadn't.

"Have you made it home yet?" she said softly into her cell phone.

"About five minutes ago. What's up, kiddo?"

"I need to come by."

"Okay. I'll leave the door unlocked."

"Well, give me a sec. I have to get my car."

"Everything okay?"

"Yeah, I'll be there in about an hour."

Mackenzie sat there for what seemed like an eternity wondering what was going on. Maybe Ken knew all along and was covering for Julian, or Ken was trying to warn Julian about the call she had placed. Her mind was so rattled that she didn't even see Ken when he came back to the car.

"You okay?" he asked.

"Oh sure, just a little tired, that's all. Did you eat?"

"No, the wait was too long. I thought I could do takeout but even that was too long. Sorry, sweetie."

"Oh, it's okay. Are you ready?"

"Yep."

They continued the silent drive home and Mackenzie hurried off the moment Ken dropped her off, packing an overnight bag and quickly leaving for Ginger's.

She made it to Ginger's flat and let herself in as the sounds of Jill Scott filled the air, along with the aroma of marijuana, luring her in.

She flopped down on the bright red leather sofa and kicked off her shoes, waiting for Ginger to emerge from the shower. The vision of Julian and Anayelica never left her.

Ginger step out of the bathroom as steam and smoke provided a great entrance. She was wrapped in her robe along with a towel to cover her long, beautiful hair. She hummed along to Jill Scott's "Let's take a walk" without seeing Mackenzie sitting there watching her.

She walked into her room, taking off her robe and towel, letting her hair fall down her back, gracefully. She walked from room to room, picking up her mess—still with no indication that she had an audience.

She jumped when she saw Mackenzie sitting there with a smile.

"So, is this how you entertain your guests?"

"You're not a guest, you're an intruder. Girl, you scared the shit out of me. Why didn't you say something?"

"Sorry." Mackenzie smiled and threw up her hands. "I was too busy enjoying the show."

Her naked body was like a picture of perfect art—her perfect breasts, cinnamon brown skin, and long, beautiful hair looked enticing to Mackenzie. She had seen the beauty in Ginger's eyes and the shimmer that whispered a language that she understood.

"Come sit, relax for a sec."

"Well, let me put something on."

Mackenzie shook her head no and motioned for Ginger to sit beside her.

"Mackenzie, I really need to get dressed. It'll just take a sec."

"I want to look at you," she said, as her eyes welled up with tears.

"Sweetie, what's wrong?" Ginger said, as she sat beside her with her bare body against the soft leather sofa. Mackenzie laid her head on her shoulder.

"What's wrong?" she asked again, as Mackenzie put her hands in her hair and massaged the back of her head.

"Mackenzie, don't. You know what I'm dealing with. I can't play these games with you," Ginger said, as she began to moan at the intensity of Mackenzie's hands on her skin, reaching at her breasts, groping her, sucking her, and pulling her into her.

"Mackenzie stop there's something I need to tell you."

The words seemed to set a fire inside of her. She ignored them as she kneeled in front of Ginger and pulled her into her, savoring her juices as Ginger lost control, pulling Mackenzie back into her. She couldn't breath, and she didn't want to. She climaxed to the sounds of Gingers moans and waited for seconds to pass as Ginger quickly followed.

"I want to feel you close to me," she whispered to Ginger, who pulled

Mackenzie's shirt and bra off and tasted her, too. She unzipped her pants while her tongue danced on her titties and Mackenzie came out of her clothes with anticipation. Ginger pulled her down to the floor and lay in between her legs.

Ginger used her strength and pulled Mackenzie over then on top of her well within reach of her vagina. They moaned together as Mackenzie rode her with an arched back, biting down on her lips. They locked hands, moving with force, trying to get to that final place.

Ginger had the strength while Mackenzie showed stamina, and keeping themselves aligned and intertwined, they fucked like two dogs in heat. There was no friction, just juices as their vaginas made a fire. Ginger rolled her over, licking her spine and caressed her ass. Stopping in between to lick the juice, she went back at it with more force.

It was a new feeling for Mackenzie. She loved the new attention from behind, as Ginger pressed into her body like no man had ever done.

"Wait," Ginger said, as she stopped and left briefly from the scene of the crime. She came back from her room as Mackenzie lay on her stomach. She rubbed her down and pulled Mackenzie into the doggie style position, rubbing her back and placing her fingers inside. Making sure that she was still wet, she put her device close, touching Mackenzie's flesh. Mackenzie moaned with intensity. She needed something inside her; she wanted something inside of her.

The hollow piece was good enough, as Ginger moved in and out, slow, and then faster. She moved Mackenzie with her rhythm. Then down on top of her, she rode Mackenzie from behind, moaning louder and louder while the two of them couldn't help but to climax.

Trembling with sweat all over their bodies their breaths seemed to hum in unison and like a lullaby they drifted off to sleep for awhile.

"Sweetie, I have to go in tonight; I'm already late," Ginger said as Mackenzie curled close to her on the floor. Their sexual scent laced with marijuana filled the entire apartment. Mackenzie just laid there with no words or movement, just Ginger stroking her hair.

"I mean, I guess I could call in, but I should have done that hours ago sweetie."

"Well go then, if that's what you have to do," she said.

"Mackenzie, that's not what I mean. You haven't said anything to me. I don't know if you want me to stay or go. I don't know what to say about this or us."

"Ginger, just go, I'll be fine," Mackenzie said, as she got up and headed to the bathroom.

"Mackenzie," Ginger called out, but Mackenzie shut the bathroom door.

"Mackenzie, I can't let you do this to me. Maybe you should leave. I feel like I'm going backwards with you," she said, with her back against the bathroom door and arms folded across her chest.

"Why did you just say that?" Mackenzie said, as she opened the bathroom door and Ginger stumbled.

"Look Mackenzie," Ginger said, as she faced her. "I can't play these games with you. You want to work things out with your husband but when he's unavailable, you come running to me. Sweetie, I don't have the emotional strength."

"You're right, is that what you wanted to tell me?" Mackenzie said. She moved past Ginger ignoring her hard stare and blinking back tears.

"Hey, hey, sweetie, what is it?" Ginger asked. She pulled Mackenzie over and hugged her.

Mackenzie began to sob as Ginger held her close. They hugged with all of their might.

"He's cheating," Mackenzie said in between sobs. "I saw him with her...they were together...Oh God, what am I going to do?"

"Julian is cheating?"

"Yes," she yelled. "You knew it, too, didn't you?" she said, pushing Ginger away.

"I only knew what Ken insinuated. And of course, there was a time..." Ginger began but hesitated, then quickly changed her tone.

"I told you because I would have wanted you to tell me. Oh sweetie, we'll get through this." Ginger held her tight.

"No, we won't. I won't. I can't believe he would do this to me after all that we have been through. What am I gonna do, huh? What am I gonna do?"

"Mackenzie," Ginger said, as she made her look at her. "You have to calm down. We'll get through this. I promise."

Mackenzie ran her hands through her hair and wiped her face as Ginger handed her a wet rag. They walked to the couch and sat, still naked and quiet.

"Mackenzie, it's whatever you want to do. My divorce isn't about you or us, it's something I have to do for me, but you are welcome to stay here as long as you need to."

"Thanks, but I'm thinking about going back to New York, or maybe Dallas. There's someone I need to find."

"Anything that I can help with?"

"No, just something I should have taken care of a long time ago."

"You feel like talking about it?"

"No. I don't know what I feel like doing, to tell the truth. My whole life is this huge ball of confusion. I can't get anything right."

"Don't be so hard on yourself, kiddo."

Mackenzie breathed out hard, and upset with Ginger's pet name. "How old are you, Ginger?"

"Why?" Ginger asked, with a confused look on her face.

"You always call me kiddo—just curious."

Ginger smiled. "I say that a lot to my patients—bad habit. I'm thirty-four."

Mackenzie pulled her knees into her chest and sighed out loud. "So, are you going in?"

"Depends," she said with a smile, "on if my friend needs me."

"She does, she just doesn't know how she needs you," she said, staring at Ginger's hardwood floor.

"I'll be right back." Ginger got up from the sofa and went into her bedroom. She stayed there for a couple of minutes, then emerged with some scrubs for Mackenzie. She was dressed in sweats and a T-shirt and held her cordless phone in her hand.

"Hi, Bill. How are you?

"Yes, I'm sorry, this medication may be too strong. Yeah that works, too, but I don't want to become addicted," Ginger said, as she sat beside Mackenzie.

"Well, I hate to leave you guys hanging. Maybe I can come in a couple of hours and stay later. No sweetie, it's not a problem—it's my job. Okay, see you soon. Thanks again, Bill. Bye."

"You gotta go in, huh?"

"I do, but, not for a couple of hours are you hungry?"

"No, well, maybe. Are you?"

"Little bit—sex and weed don't mix. If I was getting both on a regular basis, I would be as big as a house."

"You are so crazy. You have a perfect shape."

"That's because I only get one of the two on a regular basis."

"I won't even ask which one," Mackenzie said with a giggle.

"So, what was that thing you used?"

"What thing?"

"Ginger, you know what I'm talking about. Don't play."

Ginger sucked on her bottom lip playfully. "What, my little friend?"

"I wouldn't use the word *little*. That would be an understatement. "

"Who Skippy, my little boy wonder, that gives me the best, of both worlds?"

"Is that what you call it?"

"Yeah, something that wonderful deserves a name."

"Skippy? Why not Earl or something powerful like William or Richard, and then you could call it *Dick* for short."

"Oh you are just too creative, Ms. Mackenzie, too creative."

"I try. So, where did you get it, and how did you use it on both of us at the same time?"

"Secrets, secrets."

"So, you're not going to tell me or show me?"

"Sweetie, I have to be at work in a couple of hours. If I bring Skippy out, he may want to play." She winked at Mackenzie.

"Well, it takes two."

"Mackenzie, you wouldn't last five seconds with me and Skippy in the room."

Mackenzie rolled her eyes and smiled. "Come on, let me see," she said.

"Okay, but we'll have to make it quick."

"Oh, girl, please. Just let me see the thing."

Ginger hopped up, bouncing her perfect breasts underneath her T-shirt, and quickly returned with a shiny silver box.

"Okay, here he is, but I can't be responsible for what happens when you open that box." she said with a wink then puffed on a fresh joint.

"Well, you smoke and let me examine."

Mackenzie picked up the long, shiny silver box and clicked the latch. Opening it, she placed her hands on Mr. Skippy as Ginger smiled and watched.

Chapter Nineteen

"Best of both worlds, huh?" she said, as Ginger continued to smile. "I guess this is every lesbians' fantasy?"

"I don't know, did you like it?" Ginger asked, as Mackenzie admired the width and length.

"So, which side did you use on me . . . this one?" she said, as she ran her fingers across the top of the two-sided dildo.

"You can't tell?"

Mackenzie shook her head and moved her hands up and down, simulating manual stimulation.

"That's the side I used on me," Ginger said, as she inhaled the slender joint, with its scent filling the room.

Mackenzie placed it in between her fingers and sucked her bottom lip. "Show me how this works?" she said suggestively, opening her legs. Ginger placed her half-smoked joint in a nearby ashtray and walked over to Mackenzie, rubbing the dildo between her legs.

"Hurry, before I change my mind," she said, as she pulled Ginger's hand on top of hers. "I want you to fuck me." She moaned as Ginger began to pull her out of her clothes.

"Mackenzie, are you sure? We don't have to do this."

"Shhh…just put it on."

She opened wide to welcome Mr. Skippy and Ginger and smiled at Ginger as she struggled with the device. She was wet and intoxicated with anticipation. She couldn't wait for the two of them to explode.

Ginger pulled her legs up close and gently pushed Mr. Skippy inside. Mackenzie was dripping wet and felt like she couldn't wait. She wanted to feel Ginger move, see the simmer in her eyes and hear her sexual moans. It was like music to Mackenzie, which increased the intensity, causing her to climax even sooner.

She was inside. When she looked deep into Mackenzie's eyes, she pulled her in and moaned with each thrust. Mackenzie spread even wider as Ginger pushed deeper into her abyss. Her moans were humming as sweat dripped from each of them and they locked lips in a passionate kiss.

They couldn't get enough as their tongues wrestled with one another without taking a breath. Their saliva was one in the same.

"I lose so much control with you," Ginger said, as they slowed to catch their breath.

"Shhh, don't stop."

"Mackenzie, shit, how do I let you do this to me? We have to stop. This is too much."

She ignored her words and wrapped her legs around her waist, pulling Ginger on top of her. She pulled her in deeper and deeper. "Don't stop, Ginger," she whispered. "Don't stop."

As they moved together in unison, Ginger moaned and panted as Mackenzie moved her back and forth, tears filling her eyes. She was reaching her climax as time stood still and Ginger bucked back and forth like she was the king of her jungle. She leaned up with an arched back and with one final thrust, Mackenzie leaned into her and greeted her as they both were overcome.

"I think I'm going to like being roommates," Mackenzie said, smiling as Ginger rolled onto the floor.

"I'm exhausted. You're like the energizer bunny, huh? Just keep going and going."

"Sometimes, but it's late, and I know you're going in tonight. You want me to drive you?"

"Do you mind? I'm going to be a zombie tonight."

"You know I can come with. That is, after I go get my clothes. Can you believe he hasn't even called me?"

"Yeah, I noticed that, but we haven't actually been expecting that. I mean, do you honestly think we would have done this if he had?"

"Good point, but I think eventually we would have. Miami kind of set the tone for us. We were almost strangers, tearing up the sheets. Shoot, I knew then I was in deep trouble with you."

"But do you think if things were good between you and Julian that this would have happened. Be honest?"

"I don't know, Ginger. I really don't know." she said, looking at Ginger on the floor lying on her back.

"I've been with a lot of women. I'm not too proud of that either, but it's true. I honestly believed that that life was over for me, then I met you and now I'm back in the same ole shit again."

"Okay, well maybe we should talk about this some other time. I've got to get ready anyway," Ginger said. She wasn't too happy with Mackenzie's response or take on their complicated situation.

"Are you sure?"

"Yeah, I'm sure. Let me get my shower and change. I'll be ready in a sec."

Ginger showered while Mackenzie patiently waited, straightening up the mess the two ladies had made during the day. She tucked Mr. Skippy away, giggling at the device and the wonders she'd experienced with it.

They left Ginger's apartment and headed to her job, Community General, after Mackenzie quickly showered.

"You're awfully quiet. You okay?"

"Yeah, just tired. I hope my little angels are all okay tonight."

"Is it usually pretty tough?"

"Some days are better than others. I hope tonight is a good night."

"Me, too," Mackenzie said, as she drove Ginger's Range Rover down the quiet streets to the hospital.

"Well, not too many cars. I guess we'll be slow. Are you sure you don't mind doing this?"

"Of course not, Ginger. I'll just run home and get a few things and be back to keep you company. Is there anywhere I should look in particular?"

"Third floor, Wing A. Just ask the nurses' station to page me."

"Okay, see you in a bit," Mackenzie said, as she pulled up to the emergency room entrance. She leaned over and reached for Ginger's hand, then softly kissed her pouty lips.

"Thanks again," Ginger said, before she zipped into the corridor in her light blue scrubs and clogs.

Mackenzie pulled off, headed to the highway to find the quickest route to her home. She could only hope that Julian wasn't there to greet her.

She maneuvered through traffic, listened to talk radio, and thought about the latest events in her life, wondering what they meant. She ignored the guilty pangs that tore at her because she had suddenly forgotten about her child.

Her husband was cheating, she wasn't working, and thoughts of Ginger filled any space in her mind. Her priorities were definitely out of order, and she knew it.

"Great, he's home." She sighed as she pulled into their parkway. "I'm just gonna go in, get my stuff, and leave. I have nothing to say to him," she said out loud, trying to convince herself. She parked Ginger's vehicle and clicked on her alarm as she proceeded to their front door.

"Oh God, Mackenzie, where have you been? I've been looking all over for you."

Mackenzie stared at him with a *go to hell look* and walked past him.

"What, I've been going nuts looking for you. Where have you been? Ken said he picked you up from the airport earlier; that's the last he heard from you."

"You were supposed to pick me up, Julian. That's the problem."

"Honey, I just got caught up at work. I'm sorry. It will never happen again."

"You're right," she said, as she went to their bedroom and began packing a bag.

"Wait, what are you doing, honey? I said I was sorry. What are you packing for?"

"Julian, I don't know what's going on. I really don't, but I'm not going to sit around here while you do whatever you want to do."

"Baby, what are you talking about? I've been pulling out my hair trying to find you. Ken said he dropped you off here earlier, and when I get home, there's no sign of you. I've called the police twice. There's a missing person's report out on you, its 11'o clock at night, how come you haven't answered your phone?"

"Well call them and cancel it. I'm fine." she snapped, as she packed as much as she could in her tourist black suitcase and walked away from Julian without saying a word about what she'd seen.

"Hey," he said, grabbing her arm. "What are you doing? I've cooked dinner. Let's sit down and talk, honey. I need you tonight."

"Julian, get the hell off of my arm. Now!"

"What the hell has gotten into you, Mackenzie? I thought we made up. What is it now?" he said, as she walked out of the front door, clicked the alarm on Ginger's car, and threw her suitcase in the back seat.

"I'll be at Ginger's," she barked, as Julian stood there while she drove off and searched her purse for her cell phone.

"What about Jay-Jay?" he called out to her. But she hadn't heard him. She sped back to the hospital realizing that her cell phone wasn't in her purse.

"Shit." She parked in the garage using Ginger's sticker on her vehicle, then walked through the dark parking lot a little turned around, feeling as though someone was following her. She sped up her pace, greeted the half-asleep security officer, and went into the front entrance of the hospital headed towards the information desk.

"Hi, ma'am. Can you direct me to the pediatrics wing?" she asked the slightly plump young lady with bright red, straight hair and pink lipstick.

"Pediatrics is on the other side of the building, but you can get to it by catching the elevator to the third floor and then walking through the corridor and swing right. You'll be at their nurses' station. Okay?"

"Okay, thanks." Mackenzie did as she was told. Following the young woman's directions, she was quickly at the nurses' station, which was accompanied by two nurses and filled with pictures drawn by their young patience. The atmosphere was nostalgic and bright with finger paintings, stick figures, and collages filling the walls.

"I'm looking for Dr. Smallwood. Is she here?"

The nurse looked up at Mackenzie, trying to read her connection to Ginger. Mackenzie looked back, hoping that this wasn't a personal friend of Ginger's or someone that she might be involved with. The tall blonde with bright blue eyes and slight freckles smiled, showing her pretty teeth, and said, "Dr. Smallwood is in the lounge. Would you like for me to get her for you?"

"Yes, please, that would be fine. Tell her Mrs. Taylor is here."

"Sure. Be right back. Cindy, if Tom calls, tell him I'll call him back," she said, as she stepped out of the nurses' station and waltzed down the hall.

Mackenzie leaned against the station, admiring the young artist and their work while Cindy continued to do her crossword puzzle until the phone interrupted her.

"Pediatrics wing, may I help you?" her southern voice said, filled with enthusiasm.

"Okay, okay, will do, Julie," she said, before hanging up the phone.

"Mrs. Taylor, you can meet Dr. Smallwood in the lounge. It's just down the hallway on the left."

"Thank you," Mackenzie replied, as she walked down the hallway to the lounge.

The hallway walls, filled with more pictures of finger paintings, drawings, and pictures, reflected in Mackenzie's eyes as she made her way to the lounge. Knocking softly and then letting herself in, she found Ginger napping on one of the sofas.

"Dr. Smallwood is resting, but she'll be up soon if you want to sit and wait," the nurse said, as she came from the bathroom.

"Sure, I'll wait or maybe come back, it doesn't matter."

"No, it's fine, have a seat. There are magazines and the television—she'll be up soon," she said, as she let herself out.

Mackenzie continued to stand and watch a peaceful Ginger resting.

Sex and weed, she thought and smiled, as she sat in one of the lounge chairs and picked up the *Women's Journal* magazine.

"Where's Mommy?" the cover page read: children of incarcerated mothers. She stared at the bold words and tried to digest its meaning. Jay-Jay tapped at her heart. She realized that she had forgotten all about her because she was caught up *again* in her own sins.

I wonder if Jonathan has found out anything? She placed the magazine back on the table. *Guess I have to do this alone now, that damn lying ass Julian...lying ass Julian.* Those thoughts danced around her mind in between images of her and Ginger. The passion and intensity scared her more than anything.

"Hey, kiddo," Ginger said, pulling Mackenzie out of her dream world.

"Hey, girl. Still tired, huh?"

"Little bit. I see you found it okay."

"Yeah, wasn't too bad."

There was silence as Ginger and Mackenzie sat there. They let memories fill the empty space and the coziness of the lounge made them both feel the urge to be close.

"Do you believe in God, Mackenzie?"

"Of course, but I don't even deserve what he's blessed me with."

"Really?" Ginger said, as she looked over at Mackenzie.

"Yeah, but don't ask me to explain. I just feel so undeserving right now."

"How do you know he exists? I mean, do you talk to him? Does he answer you? How do you know?" she asked inquisitively.

"Girl, to tell you the truth, I should be dead. I've done a lot of stupid things, hurt a lot of people, innocent people, yet God always made provisions for me."

Ginger looked at her, waiting for her to finish.

"I still look back in awe at what he has done. Girl, I was the worst—self-destructive, addicted to vanity and drugs, oh yeah and alcohol, too. And the worst thing about it is that I hurt someone so innocent during all of that time. And I can never change or fix that. Ever."

"Interesting," Ginger said, then turned her head away. "Are you still staying at my place for a while?"

"Yeah, if that's still okay?"

"It's okay."

They continued to sit for the next hour or so. Mackenzie napped as Ginger stared at the empty wall until Julie came in for her so that they could check on one of her patients.

Chapter Twenty

"Ginger, how do you work such long hours? My hat goes off to you, girl."

"It's pretty tough but it's my job, and I like what I do."

"Understood. I miss working so much."

"So, go back. Who says you can't?"

"I know. I just don't feel like doing much of anything lately. I'm so angry."

"Julian?" Ginger asked, as they sat at Ginger's coffee table sipping on flavored coffee.

"Yeah, I feel like such a failure."

"Why, he cheated, not you—well, sort of."

"And then there's that issue that keeps playing in the back of my mind. Believe it or not, I'm starting to feel a little caged."

Ginger shook her head, trying to understand Mackenzie's frustrations and trying to make sense of her own. Her stomach was in knots as the complexity of their relationship continued to grow.

"So, what's up for today?" Mackenzie asked, changing the subject.

"Well, I have to be back at work this evening. I kind of wanted to just lounge around and relax.

Mackenzie looked over at Ginger and smiled with a flirtatious hint. "Anything I can do to help?"

"No, well, maybe pick up some orange juice."

"Well, that's not what I had in mind," she said, as she rubbed her foot against Ginger's underneath the table. Ginger smiled back, setting her coffee cup on the table.

"Have some more?" she asked with a soft smile, flirting back. She looked down at Ginger's perfect breasts, which were always erect, showing through her muscle tee, and she wanted more than anything to taste them and listen to her moans.

She wanted to interlock hands and continue to forget that she had another life now. Ginger was becoming her high, something that she needed to take the edge off. She gently stroked Ginger's legs underneath the table again, watching as her breathing changed. Her soft skin against her toes made her moist as she thought of new ways for them to explore.

Ginger rubbed her neck with her hands and let her hands graze her nipples. She licked her lips with sultry eyes—the simmer that Mackenzie couldn't resist.

"Come here," Ginger whispered. Mackenzie made her way to Ginger, instantly massaging her breasts and neck. She reached underneath her tee as her perfect breasts filled up her hands; Ginger's moans were calling her.

She pulled Ginger up and leaned her across the table. Ginger looked back at Mackenzie with smiles while she began to pull off her fitted sport panties. Her hands touched her from behind and met Ginger's there as well. They laughed at her wetness and tasted their fingers before Mackenzie turned her around where their lips met.

Soft kisses were followed by hard tongues. Still battling for air, Ginger stopped her first and said, "Come on."

She led Mackenzie to her bedroom, the site of her resting-place. The all-white room with an oak sleigh bed, white goose down comforter, and black and white photos of Ginger and her colleagues with former patients sat perfectly in her model bedroom.

Ginger led her close to her bed and reached out to cup her face in her hands as she kissed her, softly savoring the taste of her full lips. She had given everything in that kiss, wanting Mackenzie to know how much she cared for her.

She looked into her eyes and pulled her close until they fell onto one another on her fluffy bed. They laughed like two kids, then kissed and explored the taste of each other's tongues. She led as Mackenzie followed, lost in the secret sweat that began to cover their skin with wetness, waiting to explode. They were naked and began to taste each other's breasts, wrestling so they both could savor the taste.

Their bodies were sticky as Mackenzie led her fingers down Ginger's spine. She opened her legs and Ginger rested there quickly, then moved with the strength of her body and moaned with ecstasy as Mackenzie pulled her in.

"I want to taste you," she said, in between kisses, but Mackenzie didn't want her to stop her groove.

"Let me taste you," she said again, then made her way down to Mackenzie's pearl. She dusted off the edges, going in deep, while her two fingers added more intensity to her feast.

Moments later, Mackenzie climaxed, as Ginger quietly rose to her feet. She went to retrieve their special friend, *Mr. Skippy*.

She was inside of Mackenzie in no time, as they intertwined hands, making slow love, the painful love, goodbye love, which always leaves a lasting impression.

In their favorite position, doggie style, she moaned with fervor, panting until they both came simultaneously.

Collapsing down onto Mackenzie, their sweat mixed in as they both trembled. Both wide-awake, they lay there until Ginger spoke. "This is getting complicated," she said softly, holding back the tears at the tip of her eyelids.

"Probably so. You okay?" Mackenzie asked.

"No," she replied, as their breathing took on separate patterns.

"You want to talk about it?"

"No," she said, clearing her throat, then spoke again, softer.

"Are you okay?" Then added, "What does this mean to you?" she asked Mackenzie, lying there overwhelmed with guilt.

"I still love my husband, if that's what you mean."

Silence filled the room, except for the sounds that a clock makes when time is passing.

Mr. Skippy slid out as Ginger got up. "I've got to get ready for work."

"It's still early," Mackenzie said, not looking at Ginger walk to the shower. She forced her eyes shut and drifted off to sleep, escaping what was inevitable.

Her drool seeped deep into Ginger's blanket like a sleeping aid until Ginger tapped her on her shoulder.

"Mackenzie," she called twice, until Mackenzie's eyes opened against the bright, white blanket. "Mackenzie, Julian called while you were sleeping. He's on his way, sweetie."

"He's what?" Mackenzie said, as she shot up, frantic at Ginger's words. "When did he call? What did he say?" she blurted out, as Ginger sat quietly beside her.

"Ginger, what did he say?" she asked, upset. "What did you tell him?"

"I told him yes, you were here."

"I mean about us, Ginger. What did you tell him?"

"I didn't tell him anything. Was I supposed to?"

"Well, how does he know that I'm here, Ginger?"

"Well, I guess Ken told him. Don't bite my head off," Ginger said, as she stood up and left Mackenzie searching for her clothes. She had forgotten that she'd barked at Julian only yesterday, telling him she was going to Ginger's.

"What time did he call?" she asked from the bedroom, as Ginger flopped down on her sofa.

"Ten or fifteen minutes ago."

"You're just now telling me?" Mackenzie said, as she walked out of Ginger's room with her clothes in her hand.

"You were sleeping," she said, staring back at Mackenzie, perturbed at her insensitivity.

"I don't give a shit if I was on top of the moon—you should have woken me up."

"I'll keep that in mind next time," she snapped, angered at Mackenzie's tone. "And by the way, did you get that response from God?"

"What? This isn't a joke, Ginger."

"And I wasn't trying to make one. What is it with you and this gay shit that has you doing a Dr. Jeckyll and Mr. Hyde? Huh?"

"I've got to get dressed; Julian will be here any minute." She disappeared into Ginger's bathroom as Ginger followed.

"No, Mackenzie—now. Tell me what this means to you. How is that you sleep with me and get lost in some secret world and then suddenly you're 100% heterosexual. What is it? Why do you sleep with me? Mr. Skippy is good, but he ain't that damn good!" she said.

"Ginger, I can't do this right now. Julian is on his way over here. Please, we have to talk about this later."

"Unbelievable, un fuckin' believable!" Ginger said, walking out of the bathroom. She grabbed her work-bag and abruptly left.

"Shit," Mackenzie said aloud, as she hurried to fix her hair and finish getting dressed. She wet her face, pulled up her hair, and threw back on her set of scrubs. She searched for her bag for a clean shirt and bra and hurried to put them on. She put on her flip-flops and headed for the kitchen when there was a buzz from downstairs.

"Yes," she said through the intercom.

"Honey, it's Julian. Can I come up?"

She didn't respond, just buzzed him up and opened Ginger's door. Sitting on Ginger's sofa, she waited for Julian to knock at the door.

"Come in," she said, as Julian walked through the door, fatigue and worry in his eyes. The red sweater he wore showed no warmth, just hidden rage as to why his wife wasn't at home.

"What's going on?" he said, as he sat down beside her. "I see you and Ginger are becoming friends. I never thought that would happen."

"Ginger's a very nice person, Julian. You should get to know her."

"Well, I know that, but you know I don't like folks in our business. If we have problems, it's for us to work out. She knows, obviously, something I don't. Wouldn't you say?"

"Why are you here, Julian?" Mackenzie asked, looking into his deep green eyes.

"That's what I came to ask you. So tell me, why are *you* here, Mackenzie?"

"We have some problems we need to work out, Julian."

"What problems?" he asked, his voice booming throughout the room. "Baby, I've come to take you home. If we have any problems, we'll deal with them there. Not here, and not like this."

"It's not that simple, Julian."

"What's not that simple, Mackenzie? You're my wife, and I'm here to take you home. Now let's go."

"I'm not going anywhere with you," she said, as they both stood.

"Baby please, not here, not like this."

"Not like what, Julian? Is there something you want to say to me, Julian? Huh?"

"Sweetie, I love you more than anything. Let's go home. I need you, sweetie." Julian grabbed her free hand and pulled her close, inhaling her scent, mingled with Ginger's. Kissing her earlobe, he gripped her ass, then kissed her on the lips. His rugged demeanor was stimulating to Mackenzie, who found herself deeply in need of his manhood inside of her. She felt it growing as Julian pushed up against her leg forgetting about Ginger.

"We miss you," he said, kissing her more passionately. He caressed her, moving his lips down to her breasts.

"I need you," he said, tasting her and untying her scrubs. They fell to the floor, as he picked her up and unbuttoned his pants, then moved them against the wall.

He felt so good inside that Mackenzie forgot where she was and enjoyed heated sex with her husband. He stroked long and hard, grunting, touching her spot with every thrust, pulling her up and down as they slammed against Gingers living room wall. He exploded inside her as sweat dripped from his bald head.

"You gotta go," Mackenzie said to him, as she slid off of him and he gathered his jeans from his ankles.

"Come with me." he said as she turned her back to him and reached for her scrubs on the floor.

"I can't." she replied without looking at him.

Exasperated, he left without looking back, feeling like he was the failure.

Part IV:

When the truth hurts: You cry

Chapter Twenty-one

"I didn't hear you come in," Mackenzie said, waking to find Ginger still in bed beside her.

"I've been here for about an hour or so. Sorry I woke you."

"What time is it?"

"8:30."

"How was work?"

"Long."

"Everything okay?"

"Yeah, are you up for the day?"

"No, I couldn't sleep last night. I'm exhausted." Ginger turned in the opposite direction from Mackenzie and curled up, drifting off to sleep.

Mackenzie followed shortly after, drifting off to sleep on opposite ends of Ginger's bed.

Mackenzie woke up first and showered, then prepared some tuna fish with toasted wheat bread and went to wake Ginger for lunch.

"Ginger, sweetie, I fixed lunch," she said, as she wiped the sweat that rolled down the side of Ginger's face. She leaned close to her, smelling her clean scent. She kissed her cheek until Ginger moved.

"Ginger, come on, I made you lunch."

"I'm not hungry," she said, turning away from Mackenzie.

"Sweetie, what's wrong? I thought you'd like some lunch. I'm sorry I woke you. Just trying to be nice."

Ginger curled up, ignoring Mackenzie's words. She was still angry from the words they'd exchanged the day before.

"Ginger, are you okay?"

"I'm fine, Mackenzie. I've got to go in tonight, if you don't mind."

"Damn, what's wrong with you? You have a headache or something?"

Ginger rolled from underneath her blanket and stomped across the room to the bathroom.

"Ginger, what the hell is wrong with you?" Mackenzie asked, as she followed her to the bathroom, leaving her lunch on the bed. "See, you need to stop smoking that shit."

"Go to hell, Mackenzie," Ginger said, slamming the bathroom door in Mackenzie's face.

I know this girl didn't just slam the door in my face, Mackenzie thought, as she looked at the wooden frame.

"When are you going to answer my questions?" Ginger asked, as she turned off the water faucet and opened the door, staring at Mackenzie.

"What questions, and why are you acting like this? What did I do?"

"What does this mean to you, Mackenzie?"

"What does what mean?"

"Us ... *this*. What does it mean to you?"

"Why don't you tell me? Whose picture is in your window?"

"What?"

"Whose picture is in your window?"

"Sasha, why?

"AKA *Shae*, right?"

"This isn't about her."

Oh, it's not? Then what is it about?"

"You, this, us. Tell me what this means to you?" Ginger demanded.

"Ginger, I don't know what you mean."

"When we sleep together, have sex or make love, you get this look on your face that's indescribable, like you're fighting something yet enjoying it. I want to know what this means to you."

"I can't answer that," Mackenzie said, turning to walk away.

"No, you're not walking away. You love your husband but you're here with me. You have this relationship with God but you're here with me. What is it?"

"I can't have this conversation with you, so let it go, and please don't throw around statements about the God I serve." Mackenzie said, with anger filling her eyes.

Ginger grabbed her chin and pierced through her soul, dismantling any barrier she thought she had up.

"Erasmus, get the fuck off of me, Jay-Jay is watching," she yelled, as Ginger looked at her like she was a stranger.

"What did you just call me?" They stood there for a moment as reality sunk in.

"Ginger, I can't do this, all right? Is that what you want to hear? I can't do this shit."

"Can't do what, Mackenzie?"

"This shit; this right here," she yelled, while holding in her tears.

"I love my husband and that's it. I'm not messing that up for anyone. Yes, I feel comfortable with you but it's something I just can't explain. Okay, now just let it go."

"Why? Why did you let it go so far and get out of hand?" she asked, as her tears dropped like tiny raindrops from her eyes.

"Ginger, you don't understand. This is complicated. Sometimes I don't even know why."

"Tell me why, Mackenzie," she said, crying harder.

"Ginger stop, I can't do this. Okay, I messed up. We shouldn't have let it go this far."

"Tell me, damn it. Don't you think I deserve at least that?" she said, pushing Mackenzie's arm.

"No, I gotta go, Ginger." She began looking for her bags to pack.

Ginger grabbed her arm, this time with more force, screaming at Mackenzie, "No, tell me why damn it!"

Mackenzie yanked her arm away. "He's the first man that I ever loved who has ever loved me. I'm not blowing it over this shit. I've been raped, I've been beaten, molested, abused—anything some mean, evil boy or man can do to me was done. Julian's done nothing but love me unconditionally. I'm not going to blow it," she said, as a lump grew heavy in her throat.

"I don't know why I do this, okay, but I can't ever love a woman. I messed up, Ginger; I messed up. I'm sorry."

"What about me?" Ginger asked. "What about us?" Her beautiful tall figure seemed to swallow up the entire room as she stood before Mackenzie.

"Ginger, I can't. I'm sorry," Mackenzie continued to say, shaking her head trying to convince herself.

"How do you do this? What are you, psychotic or something? How do you rant and fuck like this and then walk out like it's nothing? You're sick, Mackenzie; you need help," Ginger said, wiping her face, trying to gather herself. She was falling apart.

"Listen to me," Ginger added, "that God you serve, you need to ask him to help you, you're sick."

Mackenzie walked to her suitcase and began to pack her things, not wanting to fight with Ginger anymore or hear her tormenting words. Her energy was gone and she was emotionally drained.

Following behind her Ginger asked, "How could you do this? How can you?" She lowered her voice and said, "Mackenzie, I know all about the pain, the hurt someone caused you, your innocence, my innocence being robbed from us. I've been there. I know how it feels to have your virginity taken by some big ass man, blood everywhere, and tears mixed with his sweat. Mackenzie, please," Ginger cried, holding onto Mackenzie's trembling hand, kneeling in front of her. *I'm not listening to her. This shit is over. Damn my sex ain't that good is it?*

"No, stop it, Ginger. I don't want to hear that shit," she yelled.

"It was my own father, splitting me open at ten years old. I hadn't even started my period yet. My own Momma never said anything, with her pretty ass, going to church every chance she could get while I was dying inside."

"Ginger stop, okay, just let it go."

"The first time he came into my room, I was reading, being the little intellect that they taught me to be. I'm smiling, thinking he was coming to say good night, maybe tuck me in like he used to do when I was much younger."

"Ginger, please, you don't have to tell me this." *God make her stop please.*

Ginger ignored her and continued.

"But instead, he shut the door and cut off the light, then jumped on me like a mad man. He was grunting and moaning, shoving his dick inside of me and covering my mouth, although the pain silenced me. He got up after his sperm covered my little stomach with blood on his dick and walked out, shutting the door behind him.

"I didn't know what to do, blood everywhere, and my dumb ass mother found me trying to wash my sheets in my bathtub. She had the nerve to kiss my forehead, telling me I'm a big girl now, and we would go to the store tomorrow for some things that I would need." Ginger shook her head in disbelief.

"I shut down, thought something was wrong with me. I thought I did something wrong to make him do that to me. But my thoughts didn't matter, my prayers didn't matter, because he continued until my senior year in high school. All everyone would say is 'You're so beautiful; you filled out like the perfect little lady.'

"*Whore* would be a better word, I wanted to tell them. And I bet your daddy ain't shoving his dick in whatever hole he could find, telling you, you were his drug of choice, saying he was a top-notch doctor, free from drugs and alcohol but just couldn't get enough of his *sweet Ginger*. Wetting up my back, belly, and face with my brothers and sisters. Dumb ass Momma never said a fuckin' word. Can you believe that she didn't say a word?

"I'm thinking, damn Mom, can't you suck his dick or something so he can leave me alone.

"He started giving me hush money, or gifts, so I wouldn't tell. By the time I was fourteen, he made sure I had the best wardrobe a teenager could ever want. Hell, I was driving a Range Rover my senior year in high school.

"Then he just stopped, started working around the clock, stayed in his office on the backside of our home, barely spoke to me or Momma. So I spied on him, trying to counter his next move. Humph- he was sleeping with the neighbor's son, Josh, guess I wasn't tight enough anymore.

"They say you learn to love a man based on the love you shared with your father. Well, where does that leave me? Come on, we can do this together, kiddo. I see in your eyes the way I make you feel, the comfort we provide one another, the softness that's so delicate and precious. Please, Mackenzie, don't run from this."

The apartment was silent for a moment as Ginger's words had opened up a can of worms, memories and pain and some truths that Mackenzie had promised she would never remember.

"No," Mackenzie said, trying her hardest not to break down because she saw Ray's face, his evil eyes and big black hands covering her mouth. She couldn't breath, trying to get up and away from Ginger's haunting words and her own images of Ray.

"Just answer one question, Mackenzie, one question," Ginger said, as she knelt down beside Mackenzie, not letting her leave and holding her two hands tightly.

"Do you really believe that you love Julian? Because I saw something in your eyes. Just tell me, and I'll walk out of your life just as quick as I walked in."

Mackenzie's mind flashed back to the first time she'd met him, his hospitality and the warmth he showed whenever they made love. She wiped her tears and looked at Ginger's tear-filled face and said, "Yes, I'm in love with Julian. I love him with all of my heart. It's real love, the kind that never dies, and I'm miserable without him. My past no longer controls me, Ginger, and you shouldn't let yours control you."

"What about the truth, do you really know Julian like you think you do?"

"Ginger, don't start, you asked me and I told you, I'm not leaving my husband."

"Mackenzie, please there's something you should know."

Mackenzie ignored her words trying to get her hands away from Gingers strong hold. It was a hold that she felt she couldn't fight. "Ginger let go. You can't *make* me do this. I'm going home, back to Julian."

Ginger placed her hand on Mackenzie's face with a warmth that touched both of their hearts. "But I need you, kiddo. I really need you."

"Ginger, I can never love a woman. I know I was wrong for letting this go so far, but I really can't do this." She looked deep into Ginger's simmering eyes, fighting the attraction and fighting the love.

"My childhood fucked me up. It's been a struggle most of my life to deal with this, to get to the root of all of this. I'm not taking the easy way out and blaming anyone for anything. Bottom line is I love my husband." Mackenzie put her head back down and looked at her half-packed bags. *Now I just need to find the strength to get up and walk out of here.*

Ginger removed her hand from Mackenzie's face and touched her forehead, defeated. "Don't rush leaving and be careful," she said. She went to wash up before leaving Mackenzie crying in the middle of packing her bags.

Chapter Twenty-two

It had been weeks since Mackenzie had returned from Ginger's. Julian had assured her that Jay-Jay would be with them shortly, and he spent more time at home in between cases.

Ginger kept her word, seeking a petition to divorce Ken. She and Mackenzie no longer spoke to one another. Mackenzie knew that it was better that way.

"Hey sweetie, that was Jonathan. He said they are ready to make a deal," Julian told his wife. Mackenzie looked up from the book she was reading, taking off her glasses and sighing softly.

"A deal? She's not a bargaining chip."

"Don't shoot the messenger." He smiled.

"What kind of deal?' She placed her book down and began listening attentively to her husband. Her pulse was racing because she was closer to finding Jay-Jay.

"He's faxing it over now. Should be coming. Let me check. Be right back."

Julian excused himself to his office and quickly returned with a few sheets of faxed documents.

"Let's see. Wait, this doesn't look good. They want us to pay them for taking care of her."

"Who does, Erasmus?"

"Looks like her parents."

"You've got to be kidding me?"

"I wish I were, hon, take a look."

Mackenzie examined the three-page document. "They want ten thousand just like that. I don't believe this. What did Jonathan say?"

"He said it's a done deal. Once this is done, Jay-Jay will be with us after that."

"Well, we have to pay them, Julian. I need her back with me; this is killing me."

"It's whatever you want to do. I can wire him the money today. He should get it by this evening. Are you sure this is what you want?"

"Julian, this is Jay-Jay that we're talking about. She's priceless."

"Okay, okay, I'll take care of it."

"Thank you." She softly said content.

"Anything for you. Now come here and give me some lovin' before I head out."

Mackenzie moved over and held onto Julian as they kissed while he pulled off her scrubs and picked her up to straddle him and they moved up against the living room wall. With grunts and moans Julian climaxed shortly thereafter, then he was gone to fix the mess that Mackenzie had created so long ago.

She hurried throughout their home cleaning and fixing Julian's favorite meal-baked chicken. She took clothes to the cleaners and washed clothes in between a light work out.

All she could think of was that she would soon be a mother and could spend countless hours with Jay-Jay, helping her with homework, studying, going shopping at the mall, and telling her bedtime stories like Pat used to do with her when she was younger.

Her heart raced with newer meaning each day she was closer to being with Jay-Jay and forgetting her past mistakes. This time, she would get it right.

Mackenzie's thoughts were interrupted by a knock at the door.

"Who is it?" she asked, before opening it.

"It's Ken."

"Oh hey, Ken," she said, as she opened the door.

"Hello Mackenzie. Sorry to bother you, but I came by to see if Julian was here."

"Actually, he's been gone all day, but I expect him any minute. Would you like to wait?"

"Can I?"

"Sure Ken, you know that."

"So, how have you been?"

"I've been better, but I won't complain. I joined church last Sunday." He said sadly.

"Wow, that's good. I need to get my tired butt down there to join."

"Well, you can join me one Sunday if you get the chance."

"We will, Ken. Julian keeps saying that he wants to go, too."

"Yeah, sure. Well, just let me know."

"So, how's business? Any new cases?"

Ken looked confused by Mackenzie's question. "Julian didn't tell you?"

"Tell me what?" She asked concerned.

"We sold the firm about a week ago. I've started my own practice out of my home. I'm not too sure what he's going to do. He said something about hooking up with an old friend of ours back in Dallas.

"I didn't want any part of it. I'm pretty burned out on the partner stuff."

"Ken, I hate to be the one to tell you this, but I had no idea about the firm or his plans to relocate."

Ken's face was filled with shock. "So basically, you've been in the dark?"

"Pretty much. I don't understand why he didn't tell me."

"Mackenzie, I don't know what's going on anymore. I thought you two were doing fine and it was just Ginger and I having problems. I've been busy trying to cope with her leaving. One day Julian said he wanted to sell, and we could make a killing if we sold the firm to a group of up and coming African American young lawyers. I was so distraught over Ginger, I agreed. I was suppose to receive ten grand today in my account by three, and it hasn't arrived yet. I just wanted to check and see if everything was okay."

"Ten grand did you say?"

"Yeah, it's the last of the money that we won on a case that our client had tied up."

Mackenzie's mind began to wander. *How ironic for Jonathan to say that he needed ten grand as well.*

"Ken, follow me." Mackenzie led Ken to Julian's office. "I want to check something."

She logged on to their computer and went to their banking site. She checked their personal finance section and scrolled through to see what was paid and what monies Julian had taken in.

Her heart stopped. There were a dozen entries for cash withdrawals. Some were for a couple of hundred and some for thousands of dollars. There were also checks that had cleared their mortgage company, but one was unfamiliar to Mackenzie. It had the initials AE.

"Who's AE?" she asked Ken.

"Beats me. Man, he sure knows how to spend money. Ginger would die if I ran through money like this. Well, if she were still here."

"I had no idea he's been blowing money like this. We were supposed to be saving for Jay-Jay."

"Who's Jay-Jay?"

"A very long story. We'll have to sit and talk about it one day."

"Okay, wait . . . look, there's a transfer for ten grand for today. Looks like it just went through."

"I see it. That's me. Thanks, Mackenzie. I have some things I need to take care of. You understand, right?"

"Of course, Ken, it's your money."

"Do you mind if I do a little on-line banking?"

"No, go right ahead. I'll give you a little privacy. I'll be out front when you finish."

Now we have a problem. Mackenzie thought to herself. *He's spending money like crazy, not working, and planning to move all without me know-*

ing. And who the hell is AE?

"Mackenzie," Ken called out to her while she was deep in thought.

"Yes?"

"You'd better come in here."

Mackenzie hurried back into Julian's office to see what was up.

"Take a look." The screen had a list of instant messages from A&E.

"Who is it?" she asked, afraid of the answer.

"I don't know. But whoever it is knows Julian pretty well."

"What are they saying? I can't understand it."

"Wait, it looks like a video trying to play."

"A video? How?"

"I'm not too sure. It say's that it's buffering. Here it is. Oh, shit. How do you stop this damn thing? Shit. Don't look, Mackenzie. Let me shut off the power."

But it was too late; her worst nightmare had come true. Julian was plastered all over their computer screen panting and sexing his secretary, Anayelica Moreno. "That dress," she said, "I remember that dress."

Her heart was broken. Julian had assured her that everything was okay and what she had seen was a business dinner; they were meeting clients there. She wanted to believe him because she'd felt guilty about her own sins. But now, she knew otherwise. Julian had strayed.

"I'm so sorry," Ken said, as shock overwhelmed her entire body.

"She was wearing that dress. I never forget a dress, Ken. She was wearing that dress the day I saw her," Mackenzie said, her voice filled with emotion. "I've got to go." Her temper continued to boil and Ken let himself out.

She searched for her keys with steam simmering off of her bright skin. She was headed to Ginger's work place. She drove erratically through the busy streets with visions of Julian and his secretary on their computer screen. Her mind drifted back to Ginger's place when she and Julian had fucked up against Ginger's wall. Mackenzie felt numb as she pushed her way through the revolving doors to the hospital. She had been his fool.

"I'm looking for Dr. Smallwood, is she in today?" she asked, as her head started to spin.

"Uh no, ma'am, Dr. Smallwood is on medical leave. We don't know when to expect her back."

"What do you mean medical leave?"

"Well, I'm not at liberty to discuss that personal information with anyone but family. She usually calls on Mondays to check in with us. I can leave her a message if you like," Nurse Julie said, with her bright blue eyes.

"Please, tell her that Mackenzie Taylor is trying to reach her and to call ASAP. She can use the cell number."

Mackenzie thought about going to Ginger's apartment but quickly decided against it. Truth be told, she wasn't sure if she could face Ginger alone. She didn't know what to say to her; she just wanted to see if she was okay. She realized though that it would have to wait.

Mackenzie phoned their bank and transferred the remaining monies to her personal account that she always kept, then phoned Ken and asked him to set her up with a divorce lawyer. She tried to reach Jonathan back in Dallas but was unable to; so again, she had to put off finding Jay-Jay.

She began packing her things the moment she arrived back home. She wasn't going to give Julian another chance to lie to her. This time, she was through.

"Mackenzie, what are you doing?" Julian asked, as he entered their bedroom while Mackenzie quietly packed.

"Mackenzie, what's going on?"

"Julian, I'm leaving you. Don't try to find me. I'm tired of your shit and your lies."

"What are you talking about? And what's with the nasty tone?"

"Don't you dare, you no good bastard."

"What the hell has gotten into you, Mackenzie? I'm tired of these mood swings of yours. Didn't we resolve any issues between us? Didn't we?" he said, raising his voice.

"You wish I were having mood swings, so you can keep manipulating me and lying to me? Well guess what, Julian? Your charade is over," she screamed back.

"What lies are you talking about? And if I'm not mistaken, you're the one with the problems lying. You think I don't know about you and Ginger? I had to hear it from my partner, crying telling me his wife is leaving him for my wife! But what did I do, I fought for you, came to find you to bring you home 'cause I knew where you belonged, and I wasn't going to let that sneaky bitch mess up what we have."

"Ginger is my friend—a good friend. She's never lied or tried to sneak her way into my life. I found comfort there while you were elsewhere!"

"You're taking up for her, Mackenzie? What is this? Huh? I thought we were through with that shit."

"Julian, this isn't about me. You lied to me."

"This is about you—ever since we moved here you've been like some stranger. We make up, then you find something to blow up about. I'm tired, Mackenzie, tired of this up and down shit. I've tried to understand your past, show you that I love you know matter what, and you find something else. Sweetie, I'm tired.

"And Ginger isn't as innocent as you think Mackenzie, she's not."

"I've been to the bank, Julian. I've been to the fuckin' bank—that's right. That's what I said. Now, what do you have to say for yourself? Don't you dare try to put this off on me and Ginger."

"What's that supposed to mean?"

"I know about the business, the money laundering, and the fact that you have been paying off your damn secretary."

"You've been spying on me, Mackenzie?"

"Go to hell, Julian—you and your damn secretary."

"It's not what you think. This blackmail shit is outrageous here in California. Why do you think I sold the business? They've been milking me dry. I can't work like this. Mackenzie, I'm telling you the truth."

"Where's the ten grand for—Jay-Jay? Better yet, where is Jay-Jay? When is she coming home? You gonna tell me some more lies and pretend to be helping when you're not? Jonathan won't even take my calls," she yelled.

"Let me explain. There's been a mix up, but he promised that he would clear it up by week's end."

"Julian, stop the fuckin' lies. You have the nerve to tell me about Ginger and I—please, she was there for me, better than I can say for you."

"Okay wait, Mackenzie. Just sit, we need to talk. Can you just stop packing and sit down with me and talk?"

Mackenzie stopped and looked at Julian. She wanted to see a portion of the man she loved, but there was nothing left.

"Mackenzie, I messed up. I should have told you about the blackmail and having to sell the business, but I didn't want you to see me as less of a man. You understand, don't you? I've been dealing with so much lately."

The phone began ringing in the background and Mackenzie went to answer it. "Please don't answer it, Mackenzie," he called after her shadow down the hall. "I want you to see me, understand me, listen to me," he pleaded, but she ignored him and answered the phone.

"Hello?" she said harshly, not wanting to hide her anger. She felt betrayed, deceived, and embarrassed because she had been Julian's fool.

"Mackenzie?"

"Yes, is that you, Erasmus?"

"Yes, I've been trying to reach you. Your husband said that we would be able to bring Jay-Jay out when school let's out. That's still the plan, right?"

"Uh, sure. How'd you find me?"

"The lawyer here in Dallas. Everything okay?"

Yeah, sure. How is she?" Mackenzie asked, softening her tone at the one thing that was good in her life. Jay-Jay was finally coming home.

"Growing like a vine and a little lady, of course. I don't know where she gets it," Erasmus said, laughing.

Her tone changed with a hint of seriousness. "You know, I told her the truth, Mackenzie."

"Really, which truth is that, Erasmus?"

"The one about you being her mother, but don't worry, Mackenzie, she understands more than you think."

"Are you sure about that?" she asked, scared of how things might turn out. "Because I've been having a tough time lately; I don't think I can handle any more heartache."

"What's up? Everything okay?"

"It's been better, but I know I have so much to fix with Jay-Jay. I want everything to turn out okay."

"Mackenzie, she's very excited about moving in with you. She knows that she can come to visit me anytime as long as you're okay with it. She's very excited."

"You know I wouldn't mind," Mackenzie said, as she wiped her eyes. "Thanks Erasmus."

"For what, sweetie?"

"For doing what's right and taking care of her."

"I promised you that I would, and I meant that. Thanks for letting me. And don't worry, things will be fine."

"You take good care and use the cell number to reach me. Okay? Love you, too. Give kisses and hugs. Bye."

Mackenzie wiped her eyes and re-entered their bedroom. She asked Julian to follow her. He sighed heavily, wanting to end this and just be with his wife. He rubbed his bald head and reluctantly followed Mackenzie downstairs to his office.

"I want you to see something," she said, as she made her way to his moderate size office. The cherry colored wood table that showed their reflections was filled with pictures from their wedding and extravagant honeymoon.

"I want you to stop packing and work this out," he said, as she led him to his desk. She sat behind it and turned on his computer, fidgeting with it for a while, then went to the saved files and proceeded to open up a file. She clicked open, pressed enter, and got up from the chair.

Julian looked over at her, then at the computer screen. Mackenzie had made sure she pushed the volume high so that he could not escape her pain. Moments later, his office was filled with the sounds of him and his secretary making love. He was moaning and groaning and calling out her name.

Mackenzie kept her arms folded and didn't bother to wipe the tears that fell down her cheeks. "Don't you dare stop it," she said. She wanted him to wait until the video stopped and the two of them climaxed as they laughed like they'd gotten the best of her.

"That's the fuckin' dress from the first night I met her, Julian. Bet you can't explain that. I never forget a tacky dress! Lyin' ass! I've been your fool. Are you satisfied now? Don't you ever question my friendship or relationship with Ginger. She's been there for me. More than I can say for you."

"Did she tell you everything Mackenzie?"

"Mackenzie, did she tell you everything?" Mackenzie walked out and left Julian standing there, dumbfounded.

Chapter Twenty-three

"Today will be a good day," Mackenzie said to herself, as she washed her face. She prepared for the day by dressing casually and applying very little makeup.

The hotel she was staying at was just what she needed to escape. It wasn't too fancy but not a hole in the wall either. She made sure it was close to downtown and not too far from Ginger's private apartment.

Today she would at least make peace with Ginger and then move on with her life without Julian. She would be alone at least, until Jay-Jay arrived.

She looked at the many cars that were parked on the street surrounding Ginger's building, but none of them belonged to Ginger. Still, she decided to ring the buzzer in hopes that she would answer.

After several rings, Mackenzie was greeted by a tall, handsome white man entering the building.

"Sir, I'm looking for a Mrs. Smallwood. Have you seen her around here lately?"

"Dr. Smallwood—tall, beautiful, African-American? She works at Community General, right?"

"Yes, I believe so, the one not too far from here, right?"

"Yes, what can I help you with?"

"Well, I've been trying to reach her. Have you seen her lately?"

"And you are?"

"Mackenzie Taylor, an old friend."

"Hi, Miss Taylor, I'm Jude. Ginger's a bit under the weather, but I'll tell her you stopped by."

"Wait, you know her personally? Listen, I really need to talk with her. It's urgent. Please."

He looked at Mackenzie as if he were trying to read her mind and scan her thoughts.

"Can you wait here a moment?"

"Oh sure, no problem." Mackenzie stood on the steps of Ginger's apartment building and bit down on her bottom lip trying to organize her thoughts. So much time had passed between the two of them since their trip to Miami, her divorce from Ken, and the truth about Julian's infidelity.

Her thoughts were quickly interrupted by Jude's abrupt return.

"Miss Taylor, Ginger has asked that you leave. To be exact, she isn't interested in anything that you have to say," the young man said, sounding a little uncomfortable relaying the message.

Mackenzie wasn't surprised. She had treated Ginger horribly; not to mention ignoring Ginger's concern when she told her that Julian was cheating on her.

"Okay, well, could you tell her that I'm staying at the Holiday Inn Express downtown. And that she was right."

"Will do. You have a nice day, Mackenzie," he said as he left, closing the door behind him.

"Thanks," she said quietly.

Mackenzie walked back to her car but didn't bother to get in. She decided to take a walk and just think about her next move.

She had taken the bar at Ginger's urging so she could indeed go back to work if she wanted. She just had to decide where.

Maybe I should work for myself, she thought, as she walked past numerous specialty shops and coffee shops that tickled her nose.

Her mind went back to Ginger and the idea of them sipping on coffee and enjoying each other's company and friendship. Mackenzie wished she had handled things differently and not given into temptation but worked harder at being Ginger's friend. Perhaps she wouldn't have been so angry and pushed Ginger away because she'd come too close to a past Mackenzie wanted so hard to forget.

"God, I must be cursed," she said, staring through the window of a jeweler. "Why couldn't we have just been friends? I need her friendship so much right now."

Ignoring the strong aroma of flavored coffee, Mackenzie continued to walk along the streets in a daze until she made it back to Ginger's apartment building.

She ignored caution and waited patiently until a young couple walked out and held the door as Mackenzie casually walked in. She quickly located Ginger's second floor apartment and knocked softly on the door.

She heard light sounds and someone peeking through the peephole and then the turn of the locks. Standing there, a little nervous, she waited for the door to open.

"Ginger, it's me. Can I please come in?" The door swung back at Mackenzie, so she pushed it open and slowly walked in, following Ginger to her bedroom. She was in a short white robe that covered her head as well. Her tall, slim legs moved gracefully as she retreated to her room.

"Ginger," Mackenzie called out, as Ginger went into her bedroom, shutting the door, leaving Mackenzie on the other side.

"Can I come in?" she asked. "Ginger, I'm sorry," Mackenzie softly pleaded, but there was no response. She heard Ginger moving and the sound of her sitting or lying in bed.

"Ginger, will you please talk to me," she asked, touching the doorknob that was locked.

"I have nothing to say," Ginger responded quietly.

"But you let me in. You must have something to say."

"Mackenzie, go home, go back to your husband," she said, like she was out of breath.

"Are you smoking, Ginger? Aren't you going to ask me if I want any? I've been having a rough time lately, I might say yes," Mackenzie said, hoping to get a giggle out of Ginger, with no luck.

"Ginger, you were right I was in love with you. That's why I pushed you away. I don't understand this as much as I pretend to. You were right about Julian, but that's what I didn't want to hear because I would have had to face what I felt about you."

"Ginger, I want us to be friends and whatever else we can handle—together." Mackenzie said before she realized her vulnerability.

"It's too late," Ginger said, cutting off Mackenzie's words.

"Why?" Mackenzie asked, fighting back her tears. "We need each other, Ginger. Right now, things aren't going so well."

"We can't." Ginger said, as her voice struggled for amplification.

"Ginger. Listen I messed up our friendship and I'm sorry. We could have at least remain friends I didn't have to leave like I did."

"There was no friendship Mackenzie, there was no trust, you couldn't trust me, or yourself, so just leave."

"Why Ginger? We were friends. I shouldn't have walked away, you let out so much that day and what did I do, running from my own mess I deserted you. I'm sorry"

"I slept with Julian, Mackenzie" she said, sounding as if she was too tired to go on. Her words seemed to echo throughout her apartment.

"What? What did you just say?"

"You heard me Mackenzie. I used him to get to you."

Mackenzie pulled at the door knob again she couldn't believe what she had heard, her heart felt like it was about to leap out of her chest.

"Open the door Ginger, you're lying to me. Why do you hate him so much, why would you lie to me about this? This is not cool Ginger."

"Leave Mackenzie."

"Leave, Bitch you just told me you slept with my husband, open the fuckin' door Ginger,

you droppin' shit like this, then hiding behind that door. Open the damn door!" Mackenzie said as she tried to turn the door knob and push her way in." She banged on it with a closed fist, angry at herself for being the fool ~ *again*.

"You'd better get going before Jude comes back. He'll be mad because

I let you in."

"Ginger, I'm gon' kick yo' fuckin' ass, you lied to me, and you're lying about Julian, giving me these sob stories, now you're telling me you slept with my husband. Bitch open up the fuckin' door!"

"I'm tired," she said, her voice sounding even lower this time Mackenzie could barely hear because of her heavy breathing and the steam that seemed to emerge from her skin sounded like a tornado.

"You're crazy. You can't even face me, like a real woman."

"Go, Mackenzie you know the truth already."

"No. I'm not leaving until you tell me the truth."

"Ask Julian."

"No. I'm asking you, Ginger when did you sleep with my husband before or after us?"

"Mackenzie, just leave."

"No. And I'm about to kick off these heels and kick in this door! Answer my damn question."

Mackenzie looked at the door that separated them thinking of ways to tear down the heavy frame. Kicking off her Anne Taylor heels only meant a couple of bruised toes but at this point it was worth a piece of Ginger's ass and not the way Ginger would prefer it.

"Ginger, answer the question."

"The night he came by my place for you."

"What? You went to work that day."

"You need to talk to Julian."

"Look either you finish what you started, or I'm going to beat the hell out of you, your choice Ginger."

"I met him down stairs after he left you, told him I knew about him and his secretary and if he wanted me to keep my mouth shut, he'd better do what I asked."

"What, Julian's no punk he wouldn't fall for that."

"I told him I'd let you go if he slept with me."

"What? But you begged me to stay with you, you cried, went on and on about your father and needing me. What the fuck is this Ginger?"

"It's finished and I'm sorry about everything, I really am."

"Sorry, is that all you have to say, bitch you have fucked up…"

She grabbed the door knob, turned it with all of her might and surprisingly it opened. Ginger stood beside her bed, with her arms crossed waiting for Mackenzie to make her move. In stride Mackenzie came out of her heels and lounged at Ginger. Her right hand covered her face as she pushed Ginger's face as hard as she could. Glib and limph Ginger fell to her bed, as Mackenzie pushed her head into her bed over and over again. Her anger caused her to see no other way but to end Ginger's life because she had ruined hers.

"You bitch, you fuckin' lied to me, you lied to me.

"You begged me to stay with you, crying about what your father did to you, that shit probably wasn't even true." Mackenzie wrapped her hands around her throat and squeezed it as hard as she could.

The strength that Mackenzie thought she would have to over take seemed to not exist. Instead, Ginger hugged Mackenzie until she stopped.

"Get off me, don't you dare hug me." Mackenzie wrestled to get up, setting herself free from Ginger's embrace and ignoring the look on Ginger's face and the current state that she was in. She was weary, and had a tired look about her. Mackenzie turned her back and stepped into her heels as she slammed the door and walked out.

Just as she did, Ginger's front door opened and Jude walked in with a bag of groceries. "How'd you get in here?" He asked a flustered Mackenzie.

"Look, white boy, don't fuck with me today."

"Excuse me, who let you in here?"

"I broke in. Didn't you see the hinges hanging off the door when you opened it?"

"Look, I'll call the police if I have to. Dr. Smallwood needs her rest. You need to leave."

"Leave, that bitch slept with my husband, I'll leave when I feel like it!"

"Ma'am I don't know what's going on here. I am her doctor, her caregiver, and you really need to leave."

"I don't care who you are," Mackenzie yelled as she punched the door with the side of her fist.

"Okay, I'm calling the police."

"And I don't give a fuck who you call." Mackenzie said with another hard punch then walked toward the front door and past Jude.

"You tell that bitch I owe her a real ass whippin' as soon as she's feelin' better. Hell, I might not even wait that long!"

Mackenzie wiped the sweat that dripped at her temples, took one last look at Ginger's bedroom door then let herself out. She stomped down the stairs out of breath tempted to turn around and finish what Ginger had started. She crossed the line when she went after her husband. *That bitch doesn't know who she's fuckin' with!* She slammed the building door hoping to tear it down.

The sun shining outside was a stark contrast to what she was feeling. She wanted to yell at the top of her lungs, *I wish it would rain.*

God, I can't get this right. Please, tell me what I am supposed to do. My husband is cheating, with everyone, Ginger included. And every time I get close to getting Jay-Jay back, some screw-up occurs. And why do I feel like I'm chasing a moving train. I'm about to go to jail for murder!

Her silent prayer and her mixed thoughts carried her along the neatly paved streets. Counting backwards, frontwards and thinking of any scripture that would soothe her. She made her way back to the coffee shop where she and Ginger had met. She sat at the same table, talked to the same waiter, and ordered the same flavored coffee that they'd once drank. *Another woman,* she thought, obviously ambivalent. *She was fuckin' me and my husband!*

Chapter Twenty-four

Thanksgiving, Christmas, and New Year's were a complete blur to Mackenzie, who stayed in her hotel room and ordered room service. Her mind drifted back to Sam, growing up in the projects, struggling to get by, Pat, Jun, her siblings, and Ray.

She thought of the many times he'd sneak into her room at Pat's while she was passed out from drinking or heavy sex between the two of them. The many times he'd shown her dirty pictures, asking her which ones she liked.

His thick lips moving in slow motion as he talked and stroked his penis. His sloppy, processed hair with a willow's peek and evil eyes that stole her innocence, time and time again.

The big, black hands attached to his often-lethargic body, doped up on medication helping him to function like a normal person. His goofy laugh, also in slow motion, like a character from a horror movie, made her shudder at her thoughts.

Day after day, she tried to count the many times he'd violated her, realizing that she had blocked them so many times out of her mind. She was a hard sleeper, or at least she pretended to be. Sleeping through it, she wouldn't have to look at his face, and he wouldn't have to cover her mouth with his brittle hand.

There was one memory she couldn't forget. One memory she couldn't sleep through, one memory that had never left her.

Her two brothers had come in late one night, laughing and fumbling with the front door; she was pretending to sleep with Ray on top of her. His big, black penis on her skin, inside of her. He jumped when they finally opened the door. They pretended not to see, or maybe they *didn't* see. She was a little girl, and perhaps his big, black skin covered up her tiny image.

Or maybe they were scared of what they'd seen because that meant Pat was going to get an ass whipping that night or her oldest brother was going to get his head knocked off or a kitchen knife to his throat.

Mackenzie looked down at her bare feet resting on the plush carpet, looking at the hives that crept up on her the size of silver dollars. *Another childhood memory*, she thought. *At least they don't itch as much.*

Her scary bumps, is what she'd called them, living with so much fear. She and Pat were held hostage in that apartment until Mackenzie started walking the late night streets alone, leaving Pat to fend for herself. That's when her bumps disappeared, and she'd devised a plan to kill Ray.

Sitting on the side of her bed, staring at her feet, the loneliness scared her, as hives were now on her arms and legs. She remembered the picture of Ray's face in the newspaper before they'd moved to Texas when she was a teen and the details of his blood curdling murder. He was a homeless man at the time, and it was basically a crime that didn't warrant much attention or suspicion. But she thought of her conversation with Jun two nights before and the tears they'd both shed when she'd finally told him what Ray had been doing to her. She had blamed Jun for leaving Pat and meeting Ray at the crazy house, him having his way with her, destroying her life forever.

With legs that felt like lead, she got up and went to shower. Stripping down out of her scrubs and a fitted T-shirt, she untied her hair, letting it hang loose, and stepped into the warm shower.

The water trickled down her spine, across her breasts, and finally to her feet. She thought of Ginger touching her breasts. She mimicked how she touched, with visions of her mouth there, too. The warmth of the water stirred her insides. Letting her fingers touch herself, she gently squeezed tighter and tighter, moaning while the water touched her beautiful, full lips. She licked them with desire, missing Ginger and her soft kisses. *She wouldn't let me forget, she knew.*

She lay in the bottom of the tub and let the water pour down on her. It was maximized pressure as she opened her legs wide, placing her fingers in her soft spot. She used the water and her fingers and gave herself pleasure again. Julian now invaded her thoughts.

His perfect curve that always gave a snug fit—she thought about its girth, its perfect color, and how he loved for her to pay close attention to the tip. She envisioned oral sex with him, sucking and tasting until he was compelled to come. The warm water, his warm come, made her juices come to full speed. She licked her fingers and put her feet atop the tub as she moved her fingers in and out, thinking of Julian and his curve. *It was designed for my hot spot*, she often told him, as he laughed at her ownership rights.

Her eyelids were heavy with tears as she moaned loud, needing Julian, his penis, and his come. Back at it, she moved with vigor, deep inside, across her clit, her juices mixed with the warm water, and she screamed in ecstasy, shaking and out of breath, tears flowing as she got up.

She turned off the water, went to the bed, and lay down, still wet. On her stomach, then on all fours, she worked herself up again. It was Ginger's turn, while envisioning tasting Julian's penis. On her knees, she grabbed the sheet with one hand as the other moved fiercely.

Ginger knew how she liked it, knew the spot that kept her knees shaking and begging for more. She thought about Julian's tip, the taste of it, his eyes, his clenched jaws when he was about to come.

Ginger's soft hands, soft lips, kissing her private treasure until she exploded, the strength of her womanly body, pounding her from behind until she wanted to scream.

His "manhood" of steel in between her hands, lips, grazing her teeth slightly across the tip, sucking hard, pulling with good hand motion, mixing pleasures with her warm breath, giving him the best of her, oral sex, anal sex, and whichever new position he wanted to try.

Betrayal came in like a roaring wind as she climaxed to the thought of Ginger and *Mr. Skippy* inside. *She knew.*

Collapsing on the bed, she allowed her tears to take her far away. With a headache that screamed hangover, funeral, and migraine, she finally fell asleep.

Awakening that following day, she was determined to move on. She was going have to find some happiness and conquer this town before she let Julian, Ginger, or anyone upstage her.

Her focus was getting back into law. She decided she needed to tighten up her resume, do some yoga to alleviate stress, drink green tea to regulate her, and then a long overdue day at the spa. Hell, she was going for the weekend!

She made necessary calls, did what she could around her room, packed herself a bag, and headed down to LA to get some much needed pampering, shopping, and most of all, time to adjust to being alone.

Chapter Twenty-five

Mackenzie felt like she had just graduated from law school, and it was time to find her first job. She was excited and yet filled with anxiety. She realized that in the tough world of law, she could be rejected.

Dialing Ken's cell number, she thought about his idea of her working for herself. She knew she had some ideas about working with low-income people, but she was unsure of how to pursue it.

"Ken, how are you?"

"Very well, Mackenzie. How are you these days?"

"Just fine. Bored. Wanting to get back to work."

"So, is that why you called?"

"Oh no, well maybe, and to see if you were okay."

"I'm doing all right, considering the circumstances. No sense in complaining. Ginger's going to do what she wants to do."

"I'm so sorry things didn't work out, Ken. I know how much you loved her."

"Did you?" he asked, catching Mackenzie completely off guard. She knew that he knew about Ginger's feelings for her, but what she didn't know was if he knew that they had become sexually involved.

"I knew from the way you talked about her when we were at Nick and Tiphane's wedding. You were glowing, as they say."

"I was, wasn't I? We were so happy then; I can't really say what went wrong. I guess we grew apart."

She's gay, she's trifflin' just a no good bitch Ken. That's why she doesn't love you anymore—probably never has, Mackenzie thought to herself. She realized that it wasn't her place to say it.

"Sometimes we may never know why things are the way they are. They just are. I'm a little stumped myself," she said, lying because she knew why both Ginger and Julian were gone.

"I can imagine. I would have never thought that Julian would do that to anyone. Just didn't seem like the type. All he talked about was you and one day starting a family."

"Yeah, well he blew it. I'll never forgive him or take him back either."

"Never?" Ken asked.

"Never. I'm moving on."

"So, what can I do for you today, Mackenzie?" Ken asked, as his spirits seemed to perk up.

"I need your business expertise. I'm thinking about going into private practice, but I don't know where to start."

"Well, I'm your man," he laughed.

"So, what do I do?"

"Well, sweetie, are you board certified here?"

"Yes, thank God. I took the test."

"Did you pass though?"

"Ha, ha very funny. Ken, I graduated number one in my class and was with one of the top firms in Atlanta. Of course I passed."

"Why did I even ask? I knew you were going to be sharp when we talked so many years ago at the Bar & Grill. You had a passion in your eyes that was amazing. You were determined to make it."

"I had no choice—failure wasn't an option."

"I understand completely. I admired that in you, Mackenzie. You were always willing to fight for what you wanted. So, why are you letting Julian get away?"

"Julian is a closed chapter. I'm not looking back. And quit trying to get me back with him. I called about getting back to work."

"It was worth a shot."

"Do you still talk to him?" she asked softly.

"Haven't heard from him. No one in the field has."

"Yeah, well, he's still alive because he agreed to the terms of the divorce, right?"

"That is correct, sad to say."

"No it isn't. He brought this on himself." Mackenzie was forgetting her part in all of this—leaving her husband because he didn't tell her about his employment venture and the fact that she *had* slept with his partner's wife on numerous occasions.

"I still think you two gave up too quickly."

"I know you didn't, Ken. Ginger told you she wanted a divorce and you complied with no fight. If you asked me, *you* gave up too quick." *Although she is a cheating, sneaky tramp!*

"Good observation, counselor. Now, let's get back to business. So, what field do you specialize in?"

"Civil Affairs. I did a lot of work with discrimination cases in Atlanta and also some with civil rights."

"Okay, that's a start. Let me make a few calls and put you in the right direction."

"Thanks, Ken. I owe you."

"No need, anything for a friend. I'll call you by this evening."

"Bye." Mackenzie hung up the phone and looked through the classified ads for a new apartment. The hotel that she was staying in was becoming more of a hassle than anything.

She thought about moving to L.A. but quickly dismissed that idea because she wanted to live life slowly and enjoy Jay-Jay.

She circled a three-bedroom apartment in Northern San Francisco. "Perfect," she said to herself, as she read the ad that said it was in a good neighborhood with an exceptional school district. She promised herself she would call after the lunch hour.

Ken called back as he had promised and gave Mackenzie the needed information to get started. She set an appointment to meet with the realtor about the apartment and made plans to start her private practice. First, however, she needed to find a location for her office.

"Why don't you keep the house and have your office there? It makes sense, instead of trying to move somewhere else," Ken had told her.

"I know, but the memories, Ken, and suddenly my stomach has been doing back flips. I only fear that they will get worse if I go back there."

"Are you serious? Have you been to the doctor? I mean, is it that serious?"

"No, I guess only on some days. I know I've been dreading the fact of getting movers to move everything. I'm tired, too."

"I think you should make an appointment."

"I guess I could, but the insurance has been canceled. I'll have to pay outrageous fees."

"Now that's not like you to skimp on something of this nature."

"I know, you're right. See, I'm telling you, I'm just not myself these days," she said with a chuckle. "Well, I guess I could go and take care of myself. I have to be prepared for summer."

"Going somewhere?"

"No, but I'll need a lot of energy. I'm too tired to explain more."

Mackenzie hurried off of the phone and took a nap, trying to escape the stomach pains that shot through her.

She woke up a couple of hours later and made an appointment with a local internal medicine doctor.

After explaining her symptoms and sounding as though she was going to die, they agreed to see her right away. She arrived at the local facility about to pass out with a fever and chills—and with barely any energy.

After a quick exam and an IV, the young, handsome doctor with a bright smile and glowing, beautiful brown eyes casually said, "Has your period been any different lately?"

"It's been lighter than usual and it doesn't last but a couple of days instead of five. I've been stressed lately."

"Ma'am, you're going to have a baby in about six months. You need vitamins and a better diet. That's probably why you're getting sick."

"I'm what?" Mackenzie asked, her mind flashing a mile a minute.

"I can't be. I'm getting a divorce. Jay-Jay will be here soon. This can't be right."

"Calm down Mrs. Taylor, we'll do a sonogram tomorrow. Can you come in, say about nine?"

"Do I have a choice?" Mackenzie asked, sounding as if her life was going to end. "I was going back to work."

"I know plenty of women that work and raise families. You'll be fine."

"You don't understand. This wasn't planned." *Even though I stopped taking the pill once I hooked up with Miss Ginger, and forgot to get back on it when our little affair became to hot and heavy and I ran back to my husband like I was some track star, it still wasn't planned Doc!*

"You'll survive," he said, flashing his smile.

"I'll see you in the morning, Doctor." *Damn Doogie Houser.*

Mackenzie waited for the doctor and his nurse to leave, then quickly put on her clothes and left.

She walked briskly to her car and thought about yet another change that she was going to have to adjust to. "It happened. I can handle it," she mouthed to herself before starting her car realizing she was crammed in her two-seater and retreated back to her hotel to check out and head back to her old home.

Everything was the same as she'd left it except for all of her personal things being gone.

She walked back to their old bedroom and stared at the place, wishing that the crime hadn't taken place. Instantly, she was filled with anger and disgust. Julian had once again ruined her life while he was living it up elsewhere, no doubt. She walked out of the room and into the kitchen, pouring a glass of water in hopes that it would help with her nausea, which was beginning to creep back in.

She sat for a while, then decided to call Ken. Julian hadn't bothered to cut off the service.

"Hi Ken, it's your neighbor, Mackenzie. Yes, I'm back across the street. Yes, I could use your help. Okay, thanks."

Mackenzie began to bring some of her things from out of her car, moving slowly as Ken came up from behind her. "Wow, you can use the help. Why don't you let me get this and you go inside and have a seat?"

"Are you sure? I'm so sorry, Ken, but this nausea is killing me."

"I insist. Let me help you inside." Ken helped her inside and sat her down, then proceeded to carry Mackenzie's things back into her home. He went back to the hotel and made sure everything was out as Mackenzie quietly slept on the sofa.

"Hey, kiddo. It's me, Ken. Do you need anything else before I head home?"

Mackenzie, awakened from her deep sleep, was at a loss for words. She thought that it was Ginger.

She shook her head.

"Are you sure?"

"Thanks, Ken," she whispered, as he walked out and waved goodnight.

Struggling to get up, Mackenzie locked the door and then took off her clothes to shower before returning to bed, where she slept until the next morning.

She woke up with the same feelings that had put her to sleep and drank some water before dressing and rushing to get to her appointment on time.

"Mrs. Taylor, glad that you made it back, this will be a little painful but interesting. We might be able to see the sex."

Mackenzie offered a half smile and waited patiently for further instruction. She did as she was told and waited for what her doctor had to say.

"Well, Mrs. Taylor, I can tell you the sexes but…"

"Sexes?" Mackenzie asked, with a look of shock and disbelief.

"I'm afraid so. Looks like we have two heart beats," he said, with a widening grin that made Mackenzie want to throw up on the floor. She was hardly in the mood for knowing the sexes.

Chapter Twenty-six

Mackenzie was trying to accept her new venture of becoming a mother and stopped crying as much when her belly began to hang over her feet.

She knew she could do it because she had done it once before—only this time she would be doing it without Erasmus or anyone.

She cleared all of the cluttered that she'd managed to collect with Julian and began to set up for the new editions and Jay-Jay's arrival at the end of the month. Time had flown by.

She and Ken became closer and spent almost every other Sunday together after church just talking and eating dinner, which the two of them cooked or ordered from the seafood restaurant a couple of miles away from their neighborhood.

Mackenzie put off going back to work and lived off of the settlement she'd received from Julian and alimony. Soon, she would also get child support. That is, whenever she decided to inform Julian via his attorney that she was expecting. She still had no idea where he was, and she didn't care. She was willing to do this alone.

It was a fine Sunday afternoon when Ken and Mackenzie decided to take a walk after church and skip out on eating the rich soul food that was being served after the service. Instead, they bought Subway sandwiches and sat in the park to talk.

"I didn't know pregnant women could catch the Holy-Ghost, Mackenzie. Pastor is gonna have to put out some new pews for next week service." Ken said with a laugh as he helped her to sit.

"Ha ha, very funny Ken but don't hate cause even in motherhood, I can fit in between the pews. And, all of the single women that are overweight and want you are mad 'cause I still look good." She said laughing at her own silliness.

"Yeah, okay. So, you're changing your name to Vanity these days?"

"Oh, you're on a role Mr. Ken. Don't hate sweetie, congratulate."

"No, seriously though, Mackenzie, there's something I need to talk with you about. I just don't know how," Ken said, sounding a bit sad and remorseful as the mood changed.

"What is it, Ken? What's wrong?"

"I talked to Ginger about a month ago."

"Really, how is she?" Mackenzie said cringing inside at the mere mention of her name.

"Well, that's what I want to talk with you about." *Ugghhhh, make it quick… paleeeeeze!*

Mackenzie wasn't a bit concerned. She didn't quite know where Ken was going with all of this but didn't want to blurt out anything about her and Ginger's past excursions if that wasn't what Ken wanted to talk about.

"You two make up? That ought to make you happy, huh?" *Don't trust her Ken.*

"Not quite, Mackenzie," he said, with a sadness that seemed to occupy any air space that surrounded them.

"So, what is it?" she asked, as she turned toward him. "Damn, what's with the sad face?"

"She's not doing too well. She asked me to bring you to see her."

"Me, I don't understand. Ginger and I have nothing to talk about."

"She seems to think so."

"Really, well I can't. Sorry."

"She's terminally ill. It's a brain tumor that's cancerous. She doesn't have long."

"She's what? Did you say a brain tumor? How long have you

known?"

"Well, she had her physician locate me about a month ago, then once we saw each other, she quietly asked me to bring you to see her before it was too late.

"She told me about the two of you, Mackenzie."

"What? That we were friends?"

"Not exactly. Why didn't you tell me?"

"Tell you what?"

"How close you two were and the trip to Miami."

Mackenzie shrugged her shoulders and looked away. It had never been her intention to hurt Ken, nor had it been her intention to become involved with Ginger. *She slept with my husband or did she not tell you?*

"I couldn't hurt you or Julian."

"I know, she told me everything."

"Everything? You're not mad?" Mackenzie asked.

"No, I just wished you would have talked to me about it—maybe let me hear your side before I heard it from her."

"Yeah Ken, but she was your wife; it was for her to tell. I couldn't do that to her. It was her burden." *These people are nuts he's not even mad I don't care how sick she is I still want to kick her ass!*

"Julian said something to me about it, but I was too angry to even deal with the issue. I didn't know how to bring it up to you."

"I figured that. So, where is she now?" Mackenzie asked, wiping her face.

"She's being cared for at her apartment by the hospital. I can take you today if you like."

"I can't today, but tomorrow. Just not today Ken, I can't." she added, as though she knew Ken would still try to convince her.

"Mackenzie, there's not much time. We should probably go today."

Mackenzie shifted in her seat and thought about her father Jun lying there, helpless, and the two of them saying goodbye one last time. She thought about Pat, who had died without Mackenzie getting a chance to say goodbye, and about Sam, who had gone unexpectedly. She looked at Ken, whose eyes were filled with tears and, for a moment, love. *I guess she needs me to see her so she can apologize ~ again!*

"Okay, but you have to stay. I don't want to do this by myself." *I may try to strangle her again.*

"I'll hold your hand all of the way," Ken said, before driving Mackenzie to the familiar place where Mackenzie had spent countless hours talking, sexing, and watching Ginger puff on marijuana, all the while enjoying her presence.

They walked up to the apartment building and waited for someone to answer their buzz. Within moments, Jude, the tall man that Mackenzie had blasted with her tirade and threats about ending Ginger's life opened the door with a look of exhaustion.

"I'm glad it's you. You'd better hurry."

Mackenzie followed along as her stomach began to turn and the sweat formed at her temples. She wasn't sure if she was up to this.

Once inside the apartment, Mackenzie waited as Ken and Jude went to Ginger's bedroom. She breathed out with anxiety, not knowing what to expect, staring at Ginger's red leather sofa.

She waited nervously until they both returned with teary eyes and signaled for her to go back.

She grabbed Ken's hand as he led her to the doorway, then allowed her to go in as he stood back. "Wait, aren't you coming?" she asked in fear.

"She only wants to see you."

"Are you sure?" she asked.

"Yeah, sweetie, go ahead; I'll be right out here."

Mackenzie walked into the chilled room and was aghast as she saw Ginger, so pale, thin, and lifeless, lying in her bed.

"Oh God," she said, as Ginger slowly moved her hand so that she could sit beside her.

"Oh Ginger. Why didn't you tell me?" She sat down and reached for her tiny hand, which now seemed somehow not to belong to her. Her thoughts of wanting to strangle Ginger again this time for good, seemed to disappear and her heart ached.

Mackenzie didn't know what else to say. She just sat there and held Ginger's hand, trying to make sense out of life. Just months ago, Ginger had been a vibrant, beautiful doctor with a lovely home, husband, and full life.

She looked as Ginger lay with her head to the side resting as though she had already gone on to glory.

She woke as Mackenzie stroked the side of her face.

"I guess this is why you were so insistent on smoking that marijuana, huh?"

For a moment, it looked like she had smiled, causing Mackenzie's eyes to tear up. Mackenzie knew death; she knew that it was coming.

"I'm sorry about the way I treated you,... sorry about Julian." she said, before losing her breath.

"It's okay," Mackenzie said, rubbing her frail hand and face. "Don't talk, I think I understand."

She motioned for Mackenzie to come closer and retrieve an envelope that was resting on the nightstand beside her. Mackenzie reached across the bed and retrieved it, then began to open it when Ginger motioned for her to stop.

"You don't want me to read it now?"

Ginger shook her head slightly.

Mackenzie tucked it into her purse and waited for Ginger to get out the words that were stuck in her throat. She managed to say, "Baby."

"Yeah, two actually. Who would have thought?" she said with a half smile, as Ginger followed suit.

"Is there something you need me to do?"

"Stay, until I fall asleep," she said softly, closing her eyes while Mackenzie sat and cried.

God, she's my friend, the only one I've had in a while. I'm so sorry for what I've done. I messed up, we messed up but please don't take her unless she's ready. I'm not sure if she even knows you...Oh, God, I know now why we were supposed to be friends. Please don't take her unless she's ready.

"Ginger," Mackenzie said, grasping her tiny hand. "Sweetie, you have to make peace with God. You have to ask for forgiveness, just like I have to. Sweetie, he already knows why; he knew before we even met that we would be at this crossroad. Ginger please, just ask him for forgiveness. Forgive your parents, forgive me." she said, as Ginger slept.

She rested her head on Ginger's hand and silently began to pray for Ginger, for her own sins, for her future children, for Jay-Jay, and for her husband, wherever he was, and for Ginger's parents. She knew that she had to first forgive before she expected anyone else to. She had to trust God.

She prayed hard and long, holding Ginger's hand, sweating, crying, making amends for their sins.

The hour had passed, and so did Ginger, taking her last breaths while Mackenzie held her hand.

Chapter-Twenty-seven

The funeral was small and private, with no burial, just a little prayer service before her remains were handed over to the crematorium. Her parents were there—both were quiet, subdued, and mechanical, not saying much.

Mackenzie looked at her father—the molester, sodomite, and whoremonger—and literally rolled her eyes at him. She wanted to slap him backwards and drag her damn mother to the nearest insane asylum by her long, pretty hair. They said nothing and neither did she or Ken. Many of the select few of her co-workers and maybe one or two medical school friends came by and gave Ken their condolences. Her parents made sure everyone knew to keep away from them while they silently mourned.

She and Ken went back to her place and had small talk before Mackenzie's eyelids became too heavy for words, and she fell asleep. He let himself out.

But for some reason, Mackenzie's rest was interrupted because she dreamt of Ginger and the letter. She awoke and searched to find her purse. She opened the small envelope, smelling Ginger's fresh scent, and read her letter.

Dear Mackenzie,

I should have told you this sooner, but to be honest, I didn't know how. Not to mention that you and Ken have been spending so much time together. I guess I was jealous. But I've been working on that, kiddo. You would be so proud (smile).

Ken isn't the "great man" that you think he is. In fact, he's a lot worse than either Julian is or I could ever be.

Julian wasn't "cheating" on you when we were in Florida he was trying to "fix" what had gone wrong already thanks to Ken. I think Ken suspected or already knew that I was taken by you. We were having problems. My sexuality has always been the root of many of our fights. Finally, I told him I was going to leave him before we even went to Miami but I never told him it was because of you. Although, I could not escape those feelings from the first night we hung out.

He planted the video of Julian and the Spanish girl, Ana. Yes, it was Julian on the video, but it was all a setup or "insurance" as Ken so coldly put it when he bragged about what he had done. If you can stomach it, watch it again, and you will see that he was beyond drunk, no thanks to Ken. His plan was always to destroy you two because I had destroyed us—I guess, by falling in love with you. Or perhaps he was jealous of the fact that we would never have a love like yours and Julian's. That's the only sense we could make of this, Julian and I.

Ken was also the mastermind behind the fall of the law firm—again, it was all to destroy you and Julian. Julian was forced out and made to look like he was embezzling. Ken is such a sneak (I should talk, I slept with your husband to keep you.) He knew about Julian and I, the miscarriage that triggered my illness. He knew everything and used it all to his advantage. I am so sorry. Please fix things with Julian. He loves you dearly, and I know that you love him too. We have spoken a couple of times since you threw him out and proceeded with your divorce. He has been very supportive and helpful, says he's been trying to fix things for you. You will probably find him back at home in Oklahoma.

I have been sick, kiddo, for some time now. I'm not sure if you even knew. Trust me, I would have fought you off maybe even kicked your behind! (smile) That's where the "weed" came in. I was trying to avoid the chemo and of course, the grueling pain. The pregnancy was not planned. I am really sorry.

I hope that I will see you in heaven. I've made my peace with my parents. I told them the truth. It broke my mother's heart and my father has promised to get help. Sasha finally forgave me. She's married now, with two kids, and her husband now knows the truth about her past, thanks to Ken. She was part of the big case they or he was working on! She showed me how to forgive. She's an incest survivor, too. God has always been listening, and I know that his timing is perfect.

Kiddo, I love you, and God knows how and why. We played with fire; we were both burned, but God heals all— he really does heal all.

Love, Ginger.

Mackenzie was literally knocked off of her feet and stunned with disbelief. She and Ken had become such good friends lately, and Mackenzie had taken a special liking to him, although she would never have admitted it.

"My God," she said aloud, as she made her way to the phone using the speed dial to call him.

"Hey Ken . . . yeah . . . can you come by?" she said, trying to hide her anger.

"Sure. Is everything alright?"

"Yeah, everything's okay. Can you come?"

"Sure."

Mackenzie hurried to slip on something a bit more comfortable and sprayed herself with body mist. She waited as Ken knocked at the front door. She opened the door with all smiles, hoping to hide what she knew, and welcomed him inside.

"You hungry?"

"Little bit. What about you? You want to go for a bite?"

"No, I was thinking we could eat here," she said, as she sashayed her pregnant self into the kitchen while he followed.

"How about a sandwich or something, or would you like a hot meal?"

"Whatever you're having is fine. You know I'm easy to please."

"Are you?" she asked with a sheepish grin, and he smiled back, with wanting eyes.

"So, when were you going to tell me?" Mackenzie asked, snapping him out of his daze.

"Tell you what?" he asked, trying to figure out the game.

"You know." She smiled at him, and he smiled back.

"I don't know," he flirted back.

"Sure you do," she said, this time sitting down at the table, attempting to cross her legs. She made do with just kicking off her slippers.

"Well, why don't you tell me?" he asked, throwing caution to the wind and indulging in her setup as he stood, folding his arms across his chest like he was king of his jungle.

"About how you set up my fuckin' husband and ruined the company, for starters," she said calmly, staring him in the eyes.

"Excuse me?" he asked, backing up and throwing up his hands. "Whoa. What's this about?"

"Don't play dumb with me, Ken," she said, throwing the letter that Ginger had written at him.

"Get out, you sorry son of a—"

"Oh so what, now you have a conscious? Please. You were willing to destroy my family. I know all about it, Mackenzie," he said, as he moved forward.

"That's not true."

"Yes it is. I know all of the damn details about your damn affair!"

"No Ken, your wife wanted a divorce, whether or not I wanted her. I told you the truth as far as she and I were concerned, and you know that. We already talked about this."

"What about Miami? What about being roommates? You think I'm stupid, Mackenzie? You were a willing participant."

"Fuck you, Ken. Read the letter. And I'm sure she told you the truth about our relationship. Even the part about Julian."

Ken looked at Mackenzie with a hardened stare. The truth was a sting he did not want to face.

"What about us?"

"Us? Please, you need to leave. Now."

"But Mackenzie . . ."

"There's no buts, but your butt hitting that door. Now get out," she said, as she stood, walking towards the door. Ken followed but didn't leave.

He grabbed at Mackenzie and twisted her arm back behind her. "We're not finished. You took my wife away from me. You weaseled your little, bony ass in and ruined us."

"Ken, you're hurting me. Let me go."

"Not until I'm finished. First Sasha, that Amazon, basketball, bitch, fucking Ginger. Ginger wasn't even fuckin' me—now this. Who do you women think you are? You think you got balls, Mackenzie? Huh? You think you have a set of balls?

"They didn't think I knew, just like you and Ginger, but I knew all about it. I knew about your damn past for a long time. Why do you think I didn't want Ginger anywhere around you? I knew what you were about. I told Julian that he should have never married your gay ass," he said, tightening his grip on her arm with his breath in her ear.

"Stop it, Ken. What about my children? You're hurting me."

"Oh no, I'm not through with you. Your punk ass man is gone, finished. He'll never practice law again, but you, *Miss I like to fuck with other men's women*, I'm going to show you a real set of balls."

He pulled her around and forced her back into the living room. Releasing her from his tight hold, he attempted to unbutton his pants. Mackenzie paced and thought hard about the contents of Ginger's letter. *Why was it so easy to end things with Julian? Why had she not tried to work it out?*

"Get your little ass over here. I'm not through with you." Ken had become a mad man, but Mackenzie knew she had no choice but to remain calm.

"Ken you need to get a grip! We're supposed to be friends, but what you're doing is horrible."

"But what about the video? You saw with your own eyes that Julian cheated. He even slept with my wife. She was pregnant with his child!"

"What? You're crazy Ken. Now leave."

"He cheated on you because he's no good. He had no problems sexing Ana. It was as easy as taking candy from a baby."

"Yeah, maybe so, but not without your help. That was the night that Ginger and I surprised you two at the restaurant. I knew there was a reason he didn't wake up when I made it home—he was pissy drunk, no thanks to you, Ken. Your sick ass probably put him there, too. And don't change the subject; this is ridiculous, Ken."

"But he slept with Ginger, they were going to be together, I caught them."

"No, you spied on them, used it as insurance black mailing Julian with it."

"She was pregnant with his child. Don't be a fool Mackenzie, that's why she became so sick; that bitch deserved to die."

"I can't believe you, Ken you don't have the right to say that. And this behavior here… I don't think I could ever forgive you."

"I wasn't letting you get my wife that easy. Come on Mackenzie, they're both gone we can forget all of this and have a life together." He raised his voice in agony.

"Jesus Ken, you're insane I don't know what bothers you more, Julian and I and our love or the fact that your wife was leaving you for me. What has gotten into you?

"We can't forget this and move on. I should have never walked out on my husband, no matter what. And, I shouldn't have let things go the way they did between Ginger and I. It got out of hand but it is what it is, it happened and it caused a lot of trouble, brought out a lot of pain. Some things I know I didn't want to deal with."

"You don't think I know, from the moment she saw you, that gay shit starting coming back up. Staying at her little apartment, denying me sex, she felt caged and then there was Miami. Hell no, you and Julian were going to pay. I knew hiring Ana and having that video was going to come in handy. So, while you were fuckin' my wife, I was planning the perfect revenge with a little insurance. And she was a good fuck, too. See, Ana had to break me off plenty of nights, no thanks to you! Cost me a grip, too, but Julian and Ginger fuckin', oh, that just sweetened the deal!" he said with a sinister grin.

"I'ma show you some balls," Ken said, becoming wired with unloosened dress pants. "I know how you like it."

"What about my children, Ken? This is crazy. Close up your damn pants and put that damn thing away."

"The ones you're carrying? The ones I was planning to be a father to?" he said, softening up again. Mackenzie couldn't believe her ears. She had not paid attention, apparently, to Ken and his growing attention—and obvious insanity.

"Ken, that's not going to happen."

"Oh, it's going to happen, I didn't do all of this for nothing?" he yelled at her.

"All of what?" she asked, backing further away from Ken, whose rage was beginning to grow.

"Don't play with me, Mackenzie," he said, with his short, chubby, caramel penis now in his hand.

Mackenzie turned away and went for the phone and Ken quickly followed.

"Stop it, Ken. I'm going to call the police." She reached for the phone and held the receiver close to her head, quickly dialing 911, but it was too late. He yanked it from her hand and smashed her head with the receiver.

She fell to the floor, holding her stomach, as the pains began to shoot through her. Trying to cover her face as blood spewed down her cheek, she was able to see a glimpse of someone standing behind Ken. She thought her eyes were deceiving her. How on earth would Erasmus be at her home she wondered? Maybe she was dying and Erasmus was some sort of apparition. Her thoughts were cloudy, and slowly she began to drift off as the images of both Ken and Erasmus faded away.

Mackenzie faded in and out as paramedics rushed around her, moving her and someone else. The siren lights and police cars greeted her outside of her home as the paramedic asked her to remain calm. And she did. She lay still in the ambulance alone as they fussed over her, going up and down the San Francisco hills in a hurry. She drifted off to sleep before she made it to the hospital.

Chapter Twenty-eight

"Was it a dream?" she asked Erasmus, who sat beside her bed as Jay-Jay slept.

"I wish it were."

"Where is he?"

"He's still being questioned, but don't worry, everything will work out okay."

"I can't believe this has happened." She breathed out, rubbing her stomach and watching Jay-Jay sleep.

"So, he bought you two here, huh?"

"Yeah, he took real good care of us, too. We're a little early. Thank God for small miracles." Erasmus smiled.

"Did he say why?"

"No, just that he owed you this and wanted to help me do what was right."

Mackenzie looked away and quietly thought to herself, two deaths in less than a week—and life, awaiting arrival.

"Hey, don't worry yourself—Julian will be all right. It was self-defense. And don't forget about the letter that Ken's wife left."

"I know. I just can't believe that Ken would do something like that. And what about the baby he kept mentioning? And the fact that I tried to strangle her Erasmus, maybe she lost it because of me."

"I don't know, Julian never said anything to me about it. He just wanted to fix things for you."

"Yeah, but Ginger mentioned it too. Ken even said Julian was going to be with her."

"Mackenzie, it's over just let it rest. Some things you just have to learn to let go of and remember everything happens for a reason. Trying to figure out something that only one person can answer, but if you ask, you may not want to here the truth, is only going to hurt you more. Just let it go sweetie."

"Erasmus, this is so crazy, I feel like I'm in the twilight zone. I just don't understand it."

"Well, sometimes you never know. There are some sick people in this world Ken is a prime example. He tried to play God or something because he couldn't handle being hurt. Sometimes hurt makes us stronger if we allow it."

Mackenzie shook her head, "Did she see any of it?" she looked down at Jay-Jay.

"No, sleeping beauty was sound asleep in the car," Erasmus said, nudging Jay-Jay. "Julian was waiting with her until he saw me, startled at the noise that I heard inside. I rushed in when I heard you scream, and he quickly followed."

"Unbelievable. I just don't know how much more I can take."

"Oh come on. You and I both know that you've been through a lot, but you're tough, Mackenzie. You'll do just fine."

"Pretty soon I'll have three kids. How will I manage?"

Jay-Jay began waking up. The little pre-teen wiped her face and smiled at her mother.

"I'll stay as long as you need me to."

"I'll help, too, Mom," she said, moving next to Mackenzie, the proud mom, and leaning against the hospital bed. Still skinny with slight freckles, her thick ponytail, that was plenty bushy in the back, showed her pretty little face, rounded, just like her mom's. She had both her parents' eyes and full lips.

"You will, sweet pea? Awww. That means so much to me. Look at you, growing up, and all of that hair is finally changing to brown. Soon, it will be just like Mommy's," she said, as they hugged with all of their might.

"I'll stay as long as you need; just say the word," Erasmus interjected. "As long as you need me."

"What about school, Erasmus," Mackenzie said, holding on to Jay-Jay. "You're just getting started."

Erasmus shrugged her shoulders, suggesting that she would do whatever she had to do to help her old friend.

"I can't let you do that, besides, I have to stop getting myself into trouble and needing someone to rescue me. I'll have to find a way, that's all."

"We'll find a way, Mommy."

"We sure will," Mackenzie said, planting a big kiss on Jay-Jay's forehead.

She readjusted herself, letting Jay-Jay sit beside her on the bed. They looked at her doctor through the glass window as he knocked and then entered her room.

"Well, Mrs. Taylor, the girls are okay. I will keep you overnight just in case though."

"Girls, oh my god, did you say girls—as in more than one? Did you hear that, Jay-Jay? You're going to have two sisters. Wow, Mackenzie, are you sure you won't need me to stay?"

"You may need to transfer," she said, laughing at the great news.

"The doctor at the clinic did say two heartbeats but he didn't say anything about two girls." Mackenzie laughed again.

There was another knock at the door. It was Julian.

He entered the hospital room and greeted each person politely. He looked at Mackenzie and Jay-Jay, then walked to her bedside.

"How are you feeling?" he asked, with a hint of nervousness in his voice.

"We're doing okay," she said, smiling some.

Julian shook his head, as if waiting for the okay to relax. "Two girls," Mackenzie said, as she smiled harder. This time, she reached for his hand and Jay-Jay's too.

"Girls," he said, with a wide smile.

"I'm going to have two sisters," Jay-Jay said, as Julian touched her on her button shaped nose.

"Yes, sir. Two girls will be here in about a month. That is, of course, if Mrs. Taylor gets plenty of rest and takes it easy."

"Oh Doc, I will make sure that this beautiful woman and lovely girls are well taken care of," he said, as he looked at Mackenzie for the okay, and she nodded.

"See Mackenzie, everything will be fine."

Mackenzie looked at Erasmus and smiled, then looked down at Jay-Jay, giving her another kiss. She had a family again; all six of them would somehow co-exist.

"I'm here for as long as you will have me," Julian said, as he stroked the side of Mackenzie's face.

"I'm going to need your help, Dad." They held hands in hopes that this time, they would get it right. *Lord give me strength, to forgive him, to love him, to trust him and to trust myself.*

The End...

From the author

To be quite honest, I don't know a Ginger personally. I can't say for sure I've even met a Ginger. But then again, given the light of the situation, it's quite possible that I've met dozens of Gingers. Unfortunately, statistics say that there are several Gingers out there in the world trying to survive while dealing with the issues of incest.

Incest not only affects the individual but also family, loved ones, and friends. If you know of anyone that has or is dealing with such an awful situation, encourage that person to seek professional help as soon as possible.

Incest destroys the human spirit. It is not my intent to place blame for any of the outcomes as a result of incest, only an attempt to shed some light on one of America's darkest secrets.

J. Monique

If you enjoyed *Something about Ginger*, you won't want to miss J. Monique Gambles' fictitious basketball story, filled with nonstop attitude. Young Natalie Jones comes of age trying to forget her past and follow her dreams of playing professional basketball. Turn the page for a special preview of *Ballin for Natalie*, coming soon, to a bookstore near you.

Chapter One

"NATALEE, NATALEE, YOU SMELL LIKE PEE," the group of girls yelled out to her as she walked home from school by herself, dribbling her basketball.

"You know you hear us," they yelled again, as Natalie ignored them and crossed Marcy Ave., walking down Park Ave. to her grandmother's building in the Marcy Projects. She continued to dribble her basketball, which her grandmother had bought her for her 12th birthday.

She had taken the long way home instead of walking down Stockton or Martin Luther King. There were always so many fights and kids everywhere. And the bullies that always tried to take her basketball.

"Natalee, you better turn around, or we gon' jump you."

Natalie sighed and continued to walk, practicing her left-hand dribble. She had been a loner ever since she could remember, even playing basketball with her sister in the suburbs of Newburgh, New York. She had always been quiet and taken her beatings or given one, then went back to her room that the two shared, watching TV or listening to her walkman.

"You know your song; you better turn around, girl." They were closer now, as Natalie turned into the parking lot, still ignoring their tormenting words—until one of the girls reached out and pulled her sleeve.

Natalie turned to face her group of tormentors and looked at each of them. The group of oversized, teenagers, were dressed in all of the latest fashions, matching tennis shoes with matching shirts. They smiled at Natalie then began laughing loudly. "You are busted," the biggest one said, laughing as she held her side.

"No, she smells like PEE," the shorter one said. She had a gold tooth that seemed to brighten the darkening September afternoon.

"Nah, she wishes she was me. Don't you, NATALEE?"

"My name is Natalie, and if you can't say it right, don't say it at all. Idiots."

"What? I know...I...what did you call us?" the big one said.

"What's an idiot?" the short, chubby one asked.

"Idiots if you went to class, you would know what I said. Ya'll are so stupid," she said, rolling her eyes.

"Oh, I'm gon' whip her ass," the big one said, attempting to take off her jumbo gold earrings.

Natalie didn't give them a chance to even get prepared—she shoved her basketball in the bigger girl's face, causing blood to go everywhere. Grabbing the bouncing ball off the ground, she threw it again, as hard as she could, hitting the shortest one in her forehead. By the time she was picking it up to hit the third girl, they had taken off running.

"My name is Natalie," she called out, as they ran down the street, vanishing around the corner.

She picked up her ball and continued dribbling with her left hand, going in between her legs and reversing it behind her back. She thought about going to the park to play a quick pickup game, but she had promised her grandmother that she would be home straight after school and would go to Key Food for some much-needed groceries.

She continued with her dribbling when she heard someone call out her name. She looked and didn't see anyone, but they called her again. "Natalie!"

Natalie looked around again, picking up her dribble. There were some cars in the parking lot but no people. She looked closer at a van that was parked in between two cars when a silhouette seemed to appear. She blew out hard and turned her head, walking away as fast as she could.

She made it to her building and ignored the many patrons that were on the stoops. She opted to take the steps up four flights as opposed to the elevator, which she was sure reeked of urine.

Natalee, Natalee, you smell like pee. She heard the words echo as she jogged up the steps, reaching for her keys around her neck and letting herself in.

"Hey, Grandma," she called out, as she walked into the bathroom to wash her hands before getting a glass of juice to drink.

"Well, if it isn't Ms. Natalie. Hi dear, how was your day?"

"Good, what about you?"

"Oh okay. The stories were good. I fixed some rice pudding and did a few puzzles."

"You made rice pudding? Can I have some now? Please."

"Go ahead; it's in the oven. Just make sure you save room for dinner."

"Thanks, Grandma." She smiled as she walked to the oven. Their project apartment wasn't as crowded anymore. The two each had their own room and space and lived more like roommates as opposed to grandmother and granddaughter. Of course, it was no comparison to the home that Natalie had once known.

"I'll eat first and then go to the store."

"Oh, don't worry about it. It's been taken care of," her grandmother said, with a smile that seemed to get underneath Natalie's skin.

Natalie shook her head and rolled her eyes. "I'll be in my room."

"All right. Don't you get sassy with me, Ms. Natalie."

"I'm not, Grandma, I just want to eat in my room," Natalie said, as she took her bowl of warm rice pudding to her room and shut her door.

She clicked on her television and reached for the remote control. Surfing until she found ESPN, she sat on the bed to eat her favorite snack. She ignored the telephone ringing and watched the preseason women's basketball polls that were showing.

Her grandmother knocked on the door. "Natalie, it's Mike on the phone."

"Tell him I'll be down in thirty minutes." Her grandmother gave her a look, and she reached over for her phone.

"Yes, can I help you?... I'm not playing, can I help you.?"

"Okay, okay...I'm just joking. Yeah, I'll be downstairs in about thirty minutes. Okay twenty. Come on, I'm a girl—I have to wash my face and stuff. You know. Okay, fifteen. I promise."

Natalie ate the rest of her rice pudding, washed her face, and changed into her basketball sweats and a loose T-shirt with the sleeves cut off. She washed out her bowl and kissed her grandmother on the cheek, then grabbed her basketball.

"Yes, Grandma, I'll be in way before they start shooting," she said, as she left their apartment.

She ran down the steps and jumped down the outside steps, then took off running to the back park just in time to see Mike walking on the court, looking at his stopwatch.

"You really need to lose that dumb thing, Mike."

"You wish," he said, motioning for Natalie to throw him the ball.

"Twenty-one. Come on, let's go. My ball first."

"Cheater," she said, as she went to guard him and he shot the ball in the basket before she could even get set.

"You make me sick," she said, as she threw the ball back at him with all her might.

"Stop whining and play," he said, this time dribbling in front of her as she tried to get the ball, then pulling up for another jump shot.

"What is that? That's not defense, Natalie. You're just standing there."

"Mike, today I'm not in the mood. Just play."

"Is that what you're going to say when you have to try-out next year for high school? I told you, that's when things get serious. Jr. High school ball ain't nothin', and you know it. You not gon' score fifty points in high school."

Natalie turned around to walk away. She wasn't in the mood for Mike's tough love; she just wanted to play.

"Natalie, we ain't finished."

"I'm finished," she yelled out, until she saw her nightmare walking and singing at the top of her lungs. She shook her head and turned back around to face Mike, standing there with his bowed legs, grey sweats, a matching grey T-shirt. He sported clean, white, high-top Nikes and a smile that showed off his pearly white teeth against his pretty chocolate skin and low hair cut.

His muscles showed through his shirt. Already in high school and trying to make it on the senior team, the 6'3 guard spent most of his afternoons and summers training with Natalie, working on fundamentals, improving his shot, and helping her to become one of the best defenders for her age group.

"New rules, my ball first, and we go to fifteen," she said, asking for the ball. He checked it to her and that was all she needed. She worked Mike like never before, making him chase her and then pull up for several jump shots, sometimes out rebounding him for the ball.

She sweated like a pig and refused to let up or look at the sideshow that was taking place on the outside of the court.

Not even the screams would allow her to let up when the young woman was being dragged by her hair. The man yelled at her and spit in her face before knocking her down. Natalie saw it all from the corner of her eyes.

"I hate being embarrassed," she said, as she beat Mike for the first time, 16-14.

"We not finished," he said with an attitude.

"I'm finished," she said, as she grabbed the ball from his hand and walked off the court.

If you enjoyed *Something about Ginger*, you won't want to miss J. Monique's latest novel, *Broken Ladder*, Rebekah Claude Moore an up coming writer struggles to find true love. After a two year battle with major depression her new literary agent brings a sense of hope that things are finally looking up. The question is at what cost? Turn the page for a special preview of *Broken Ladder*, coming soon, to a bookstore near you.

She Walks in...

Chapter One

Two years had passed and still there were no words. No words dancing on my laptop screen or juggling in my head. Gone was the steadfast pecking of keys as I finished a novel or an impromptu poem. There was only one culprit for such a travesty—Burnout! Or perhaps it was exhaustion from a meaningless job that zapped more energy than the impact from a nuclear missile hitting a stack of hay. Not to mention spending countless hours with my therapist and psychiatrist trying to find reasons as to why suddenly I had lapsed into never ever land.

Up until this point my life was fairly good. I had written a couple of novels that kept my bills paid was physically fit and not involved with anyone. My job at the time, an editor for an off beat, culturally diverse newspaper was perfect.

In between book signings and signing off on bylines and editorials, life just seemed to fall into place quite naturally.

Dreadlocked, slender, bi-racial with all of the right curves in all of the right places I lived quite simplistically. I was able to hold my own in my chosen profession and at a time nothing seemed to bother me.

I have a tough time figuring how and when things took such a drastic turn and I loathed going into the office or doing anything that reminded me of work. At one point I thought it was my chief editor that seemed to work my nerves with his haughty, pretentious, overbearing presence whenever he walked into the room.

Then again it could be the doorman that seemed to get underneath my skin like nails across a chalk board. Acting as though we owed him for opening the door each morning and evening when I was more than certain he was compensated quite well.

His same tired uniform, stale breath and uncombed hair which was no doubt unwashed too drove me nuts!

And I dare not leave out the young know it all recent gradates from SMU, (some of my mother's former students) UT and every other prestigious university of the fifty states that pissed me off with their simple stories and weird ideals. I took pleasure in shooting down their stories which was probably my only solace. Not too mention their ass kissing that made them think that was all they needed to get ahead.

At the tender age of thirty six and not looking a day over twenty-four (even on a bad day) I was hardly in the mood for their far-fetched stories and questionable research tactics or better yet their character and absence of integrity.

My therapist seemed to think that I was too happy being single and I needed to get laid. A lesbian by choice and not birth, I was content on being single, saving my money, doing small investments deals and writing until my heart was content (until recently). I didn't need the emotional rollercoaster that seemed to accompany many of my other relationships. As a matter of fact it had been seven years since I sent my last partner on her way with tuition and her new lover who I was sure was going to beat the hell out of her one day.

I was a natural loner anyway being an only child with no-step siblings, questionable kin, crazy relatives or dysfunctional parents. Both my parents were stable, hardworking individuals that showed me the importance of stability and family harmony. My mother was Jewish and my father Jamaican. My white side and I were extremely close as we were studious and took very seriously our heritage and roots that traced all the way back 18th century Jewry. And as far as my folks still in Mandeville, Jamaica I remember clearly the wild parties that were full of fun with the natives bumping and grinding to the smooth reggae and soca rhythms all through the night. Just thinking about Jamaica brings about a sense of peace and relaxation: the seemingly endless white sand beaches, the lush countryside bathed in magnificent sunlight, smiling folk peddling their wares by the roadside and saying "no problem man" making you almost believe it's true.

........and the food, what excellent cuisine! Escoveitched red snapper, festival, ackee and salt fish, pineapples, juicy mangoes and sweet sugar cane from which white rum is made.

So, when I came home from my freshman year in college, wide eyed and talking non-stop about some girl (Mackenzie) that I was sure at the time I was only infatuated with, they discussed my experience with me, told me to practice safe sex and sent me back to college life. They raised a lady, no matter who I decided to sleep with and I have honored all that they taught me ever since (except a brief lapse in my choices, choosing low rent, needy, bad credit unstable women my way). Seven years of being single was heaven sent.

I was about to turn thirty seven, my sex life was nonexistent and more than likely menopause was not too far away. And in spite of what my therapist suggested, I felt no need for any wild one night stands, one sided relationships or being the sole bread winner of any union!

But in attempts to rid myself of being glued to both my therapist and psychiatrist's state of the art sofas, I was going to get myself out of this funky mood and take myself to the local bar the one I call Cheers for Women *Suz*. I decided against the private scene because it would do nothing for my mood to hang with a bunch of folk who probably had more issues than me.

I dressed rather quickly so wouldn't change my mind and took up a game of pool and sipped on Patron' and peach schnapps. My buzz was felt almost immediately and I thought about how good life truly was. I was a professional with savings, easy on the eyes and able to hold a decent conversation.

However my words seemed to get caught in my throat when she walked in. Her side profile and long tresses down her back even made me do a double take. I mean really how is someone beautiful from the side?

Creamy, milky skin with distinctive features—penetrating eyes, pointy perfect lips that were a soft pink, glazed slightly with a smile that set me afire. She was captivating as she walked with confidence and sex appeal with her friends in tow. Which one was she giving that entire ass to? Beyond a reasonable doubt, I knew someone that sexy, had to be taken.

I got back to the pool shark and continued receiving my ass whipping, and then excused myself to the ladies room. A mess of toilet tissue, an overflowing sink was a minor nuisance considering mystery girl was standing in the mirror on the phone in a deep conversation, running her hands through her hair. She nodded as did I and hurried to get out of there after using the restroom.

It was at that moment that I began to dream, dream like it was my last dream and hope like I had never hoped before. I hoped that I could change her mind and make her mine. Our first kiss would be initiated by her; she'd grab me and kiss me like I'd never been kissed before. I'd touch her in ways that talked a special language and during our first kiss, my tongue would savor the taste of her breast. Time would get away from us and the next time we would meet, I'd touch her allowing my fingers to explore knowing that just that easy we could simply fuck. I'd stop and back away. ('Cause I hate it when women give it up so easy~ it just turns me off.)

This young one I wanted to wait for until we could have sex and then make love. I wanted to love her. I had to hope.

www.ingramcontent.com/pod-product-compliance
Lightning Source LLC
LaVergne TN
LVHW091544060526
838200LV00036B/700